AND THEN CAME PAULETTE

BARBARA CONSTANTINE

AND THEN CAME PAULETTE

Translated from the French by
Justin Phipps

MACLEHOSE PRESS
QUERCUS · LONDON

First published in the French language as *Et puis, Paulette* . . .
by Barbara Constantine, by Editions Calmann-Lévy in 2012
First published in Great Britain in 2014 by

MacLehose Press
an imprint of Quercus
55 Baker Street
7th Floor, South Block
London W1U 8EW

This book is supported by the French Ministry of Foreign Affairs, as part of the Burgess
programme run by the Cultural Department of the French Embassy in London

Liberté • Égalité • Fraternité
RÉPUBLIQUE FRANÇAISE

A CIP catalogue record for this book is available
from the British Library.

ISBN (HB) 978 0 85705 242 1
ISBN (Ebook) 978 1 78206 099 4

10 9 8 7 6 5 4 3 2 1

Designed and typeset in Albertina by Libanus Press Ltd, Marlborough
Printed and bound in Great Britain by Clays Ltd, St Ives plc

To Renée and Robert – my former neighbours

To Alain – my new neighbour

Mahault, five and three quarters, hands a freshly picked bunch of flowers to her little neighbour. "Here you are, keep them, then when your parents die you can put them on their grave."

(Mahault, my granddaughter, wanting to share her knowledge.)

"One testicle in the soup is a cock-up; two and you've got a recipe."
Nadada, Franz Bartelt (Editions La Branche, 2008), quoted in *Pas Mieux*, Arnaud Le Guilcher, Stéphane Million, ed. (Pocket, 2012)

1

GAS PROBLEMS

Ferdinand was concentrating on his driving; nose pressed to the windscreen and stomach propped against the steering wheel. The needle didn't budge: fifty was the perfect speed. Not only was he saving on petrol, he also had time to admire the view, watch the landscape unfold. Above all, no risk of an accident should he have to stop for any reason.

And there and then, right in front of him, a dog, running. Instinctively he braked. His tyres screeched. Gravel flew. The shock absorbers squealed. The car pitched forward and ended up stationary in the middle of the road.

Ferdinand leaned out of the car window.

"Where are you off to then, boy? Looking for a bit of skirt, I'll bet."

The dog leaped aside, raced past, then stopped in the ditch a little further up and crouched in the grass. Ferdinand pulled himself out of the car.

"Hold on, aren't you the neighbour's dog? What are you doing here all on your own?"

He approached, gently holding out his hand, and patted its head. The dog trembled.

After a while, finally won over, it agreed to follow him.

Ferdinand made it jump into the back of the car and then drove off again.

When he reached the turning to a dirt road he opened the car door. The dog got out, but – whimpering – came over and stood right by his legs, apparently frightened. Ferdinand pushed open the little wooden gate.

"Go on, in you go!"

Still whining, the dog crept along, sticking close to him. He went up the path between two scrubby hedges and arrived at a little house. The door was ajar.

"Hello!" he shouted. "Anyone there?"

No reply.

He looked round. Nobody. He pushed open the door. At the back of the room, in the half-light, he could make out a figure lying stretched out on the bed. He called. No movement. He sniffed the air. It stank in there. Sniffed again. Uh-oh! Gas. He ran over to the cooker, screwed the knob back on the cylinder and went up to the bed.

"Madame, Madame!"

He started to pat the lady's cheeks. Gently at first, then, as she didn't respond, more forcefully. The dog yapped, jumping up and down round the bed. Ferdinand was panicking too. He slapped her hard, shouting at her to wake up. A frenzy of barking and shouting.

"Madame Marceline!"

Woof!

"Open your eyes!"

Woof, woof!

"Wake up!"

Finally she gave a little moan.

Ferdinand and the dog both sighed with relief.

2

FIVE MINUTES LATER
AND THINGS ARE LOOKING UP

Marceline had got her colour back and was insisting on offering him something. It wasn't every day she had visitors. Although they were neighbours, it was the first time he had set foot in her house. A cause for celebration? Ferdinand kept saying he wasn't thirsty, he had just popped in to return her dog, but she got up all the same, staggered over to the dresser, took out a bottle of plum wine and said she'd like him to try some. It was the first time she'd made it. Would he tell her what he thought? He nodded. She started to pour him a glass, then stopped and asked anxiously if he had to drive. He replied that he was on his way home; it was only five hundred metres away; he could do it in his sleep. Reassured, she finished pouring the drink. He had barely wet his lips when suddenly she had a dizzy spell. She slumped into a chair, clutching her head in her hands. Ferdinand, embarrassed, fixed his eyes on the oilcloth, sliding his glass along the lines and squares. He didn't dare drink or speak. After a long silence he asked her, almost in a whisper, if she wanted him to drive her to the hospital.

"Why?"

"To get you looked at."

"But it's only a headache."

"Yes, but there's the gas . . ."

"Yes."

"That's not good."

"No."

"There can be side effects."

"Such as?"

"Vomiting, I believe."

"Oh right. I didn't know."

Another long silence. She kept her eyes closed. He took the opportunity to have a look around. The room was small, dark and unbelievably cluttered. It made him realise his own house was exactly the opposite: the place was so empty, it practically echoed. The thought depressed him; he went back to staring at the oilcloth on the table. Eventually he said:

"I don't like poking my nose in other people's business, Madame Marceline, you know that. But is it because things are difficult at the minute, that you left . . ."

"Left what?"

"The gas . . ."

"What about it?"

"Well . . ."

Not easy for Ferdinand, intimate subjects were not his cup

of tea. But he felt he had to say something. At first he stalled, hinting at what he meant, talking without really saying anything. (He was a fan of the phrase 'reading between the lines'.) He was so convinced that words betray thoughts, he preferred to leave it to intuition. Though of course, that had often let him down. One thing led to another. He had a fear of unleashing a gush of emotion, floods of tears or secrets he didn't want to know. He didn't like that. Life would be so simple if everyone just tried to work things out for themselves.

With his wife he had a trick to avoid getting trapped in over-intimate discussions: as soon as he saw her going down that road he would mention the past. A single, innocent word was enough. And hey presto, he hardly needed to listen at all. His poor wife, she loved to chat. About anything and nothing. She went on and on. But what she liked most was to talk about the past. Her youth. How in the old days things were so much better and more beautiful. Especially before they got to know each other. She always ended up furiously listing the other places where she might have lived: America, Australia, or Canada perhaps. And why not? It could have happened. If only he hadn't asked her for a dance, hadn't murmured those sweet nothings, hadn't held her so tight at that bloody awful dance on the fourteenth of July. If only.

He didn't mind. He had also had his dreams. And sweet ones they were too. But he soon understood that dreams and love, they weren't for him this time around. Perhaps he wasn't cut out for it. Or it would happen some other time. In another life maybe, like cats.

So, back to the present.

He was at his neighbour's house. She had a problem she didn't seem to want to talk about, in spite of his gentle prodding. He didn't know much about her. Just that she was called Marceline and sold fruit and vegetables and honey at the market. She seemed a bit foreign. Russian or Hungarian perhaps? One of those eastern countries anyway. She hadn't been here long. Some years though. Six, seven? Long enough . . .

He looked around again and this time noticed there was no water heater above the sink. No fridge, no washing machine, no telly. None of your mod cons. Just like when he was a child. Only the radio to keep up with the news, and cold water in the sink for washing. In winter he had always looked for a way to get out of it. And the chores . . . helping take the stiff, frozen washing out of the bucket and wringing it out with his chapped fingers. Christ, what a shit time it had been in those days! He wondered whether in reality poor old Madame Marceline had had enough of this life. The hardship, the hassle. She must have lost heart. And so far away from her own country and family too. It was quite possible that was the reason . . .

He sensed there was no getting round it. He'd have to do it, force himself to talk. About stuff that wasn't just the weather. There was always her dog. What a clever dog! You're so lucky to have one like that. The last one I had was stupid but very affectionate. Whereas this one . . . Oh it's a bitch, is it? Are you sure? I hadn't noticed . . .

He took a deep breath. And went for it. Straight out, just like that, he told her he understood. He had felt like doing the same himself once or twice. In fact, to be totally honest, three or four times. But he'd taken his time, thought about it first. And found good reasons not to go through with it. Such as . . . well, off the top of his head he couldn't think of anything. Oh yes, of course, he was such a fool, his grandkids. Grandchildren were wonderful. It was exciting and so different from your own. Yes, they really were. Sweeter, livelier, and much more intelligent. Perhaps it was the way things were now, times had changed. Unless we get more patient as we get older, it's possible . . . Oh, you don't have any grandchildren? No little ones? Ah. That's a pity. But there are other things. Let me think . . .

She looked up and stared at the ceiling.

He scratched his head, desperate to come up with something.

"You know, sometimes it's important to remember there are other people are worse off than you. It keeps you grounded, if you like. Gives you a sense of perspective. Sometimes you need that, don't you think?"

She seemed to be somewhere else. He tried to make a joke of it.

"As no-one's ever been over there and come back to tell

us if things are any better, maybe it's not worth getting ahead of ourselves, eh, Madame Marceline? Better to wait and see, don't you think?"

He chuckled and waited for her reaction. But none came.

There was good reason to be worried. He leaned over. "Can you understand me when I'm talking to you? Maybe there are words you don't . . ."

She pointed towards the pipe on the gas cooker and said with a slight tremor in her voice that she'd finally worked it out. Mo-je, her old cat, was to blame. He'd been missing for days. Maybe he was dead – oh no, please, not that; it would break her heart – and in the meantime, it had been chaos here. The mice did as they pleased. Dancing round endlessly. Day and night. In the cupboards, the larder, and under the bed. They never stopped. Nibbling, nibbling away. She thought she was going mad. If it went on like that they'd end up climbing onto the table and eating from her plate. They were so cheeky, those little creatures.

Ferdinand had switched off, he was barely listening. The poor woman was rambling. Must be the gas. Her stories of dead cats and dancing mice made no sense, he couldn't make head or tail of them. He watched her as she spoke, looking down at her beautiful, damaged hands. That's what happens when you grow things, he thought. She ought to take better care of them, put on some cream. That would help. But she seemed younger than he'd imagined. Sixtyish?

Suddenly she stood up. Taken aback, he did the same. She

told him she found it really annoying talking to herself. Anyway she felt better now. He could go, thanks for everything, she would have a lie down and get some rest. The gas had made her dizzy. Ferdinand looked at the clock: four-thirty. A bit early to be going to bed. He was surprised. She told him she wouldn't come with him, he could find his way alright on his own. He agreed, suppressing a faint smile. No chance of getting lost in a house with only one room. He patted the dog's head. Right you are, Madame Marceline, cheerio. Don't hesitate to give me a ring if you need anything. Thanks, yes, I'll do that. She shrugged, grumbling to herself: I will once I get the phone connected . . .

Going back to his car Ferdinand tried to piece together what had just happened: this lady, who had nearly gassed herself, had been living for years in the tiny house next door; he must have passed her hundreds of times – on the road, in the post office, or at the market – but they'd hardly exchanged a word, except to talk about the weather, or how the honey was that year . . . And now out of the blue he'd met her dog, or rather her bitch . . . and if he hadn't stopped on the road to bring it back, then – no doubt about it – Madame Marceline would be dead by now. With no-one there to care.

Shit. Not a nice thought.

He got into his car and pulled away. He told himself he hadn't really helped her. Too bad, he would try to drop in again tomorrow or some other day. Give her his verdict on the plum wine. Great stuff, Madame Marceline, and your first time too!

In the past his late wife, Henriette, used to make it, but it had never been as good as that. No, no, I promise you, I mean it . . .

In her little house Marceline lay down. Her head didn't hurt quite as much now. She could think.

He was a funny one, that Ferdinand. Never drew breath the whole time! It made her head spin. She hadn't really understood everything. All that stuff about perspective, for example – why had he started going on about that? He must be very depressed; it seemed like he needed to open up a bit. It was a little embarrassing, but hearing him out was the least she could do. In any case it had been nice of him to bring the dog back. She must remember to thank him next time. A jar of honey perhaps; he might like that. And then, suddenly, the memories came flooding back. She recalled the man's wife. Oh my, not at all nice. Horrible, in fact. That had been at the beginning when she knew nothing and no-one. The animals were hungry and she was too. She had helped herself to things from the garden. And then of course she had started growing her own vegetables. So she could feed herself and maybe earn a bit of money. While she thought about what to do next. But in spite of all her hard work the first year had been a disaster. Even fully grown her carrots were no bigger than radishes and her onions were tiny. And every week Madame Henriette would turn up, stop by her stall at the market, and look down her nose as she inspected the produce. The following year things had improved: her carrots started to look like carrots;

her leeks were no longer like spring onions. And that Henriette had started to buy a few things every now and then. But each time she gave the impression she was doing it for charity. She would have liked to send her packing. But she was in no position to do so. Yes, she really couldn't stand that woman.

Couples, they were always a puzzle, she thought. It had been just the same with her, though she didn't really want to think about that. It was such a long time ago, another life. She didn't really know Henriette and Ferdinand, but she wondered how two such ill-suited people could have spent all their lives together. How come they hadn't parted the instant the passion cooled? Well, it wasn't that interesting. And anyway, on the face of it he seemed different. Under that rather stiff, distant exterior he looked O.K. With that deep wound inside, which he took so much trouble to conceal, he was quite endearing. When he talked about his grandchildren you could see he missed them and hadn't yet got used to their leaving. It must have been a shock, finding himself all alone in that big, empty farmhouse.

Poor old man. Not an easy life.

At nightfall Marceline got up, her headache gone. First, she checked the gas pipe, which had been nibbled away by the mice. There was still a good bit left. She managed to fix it and then put on some soup to heat.

3

AN EARLY MORNING PRESENT

Ferdinand woke the following morning with a cry of "Sugar!" For some time he had been making great efforts to clean up his language – that was the excuse his daughter-in-law, Mireille, used to stop him seeing the grandchildren. So when he realised the sheets were soaking wet he shouted "Sugar!" He must have had the same dream as on the previous three nights. The one where he swam like a fish in warm, blue waters, with his mates the dolphins. The only ones he had ever seen were on telly, in wildlife documentaries. And that wasn't the end of it. Still half awake, like every morning, he felt around the bed with his left foot for the missing slipper. When his toes finally came across something soft and warm instinctively he got up to put it on. Then he shouted "Fucking Hell!" But perhaps on this occasion that was permissible, as he had trodden on a corpse. The daily mouse: a present from his cat. Or to be more precise, the kitten belonging to his beloved grandchildren. Mireille had developed an allergy to its fur just two days before they moved out, so he had been forced to agree to look after it. Yes, it was all sorted, their papi, Ferdinand, would take care of the darling cat. Don't you worry.

And you can come and see him whenever you want. O.K.? Now run along, my Lulus, please don't cry.

He would have preferred a dog. Even though six months earlier he had sworn he would never have another. Velcro was utterly stupid, totally disobedient and a pretty average guard dog. But he was so affectionate and that made up for everything. Oh he really missed that dog. With cats it was straightforward; he didn't like them. Deceitful, sly, thieves and all that. Alright for catching mice and rats. If you found a good one . . . But as for doing what they were told, no chance. They chose when they wanted to be affectionate, and that might be never.

So the very same evening that they all moved out the bundle of fur made itself at home on his bed. He didn't have the heart to shoo it away, it was so tiny . . . The following day it was under the eiderdown, huddling up close to him, its nose nestling in his ear, sweet as anything. By the fourth evening it was sharpening its claws on the legs of the armchair, without feeling the slightest emotion or pang of conscience. And come the end of the week it was eating at the table from a bowl with its name on. The only thing missing: a napkin ring.

Soon it would be two months since his son Roland, Mireille and their two children had moved out of the farmhouse. Two months that Ferdinand had been living on his own with the cat. And there were days when he wondered – not without some surprise – whether he could have lived through the upheaval, the sadness, without little Chamalo there at his side.

Another huge source of surprise had been the changes in his character. He had always been rather a cold bloke, unshakeable, solid as a rock. No more. From one day to the next he became vulnerable. Capable of crying over nothing, worrying about everything. A chink in his armour. Gaping hole, more like. That he did everything he could to seal.

He didn't, of course, want to talk to anyone about any of this. He had never been much good at expressing himself, still less talking about his emotions. To him it felt like stripping off in the main square on market day. No thanks! He preferred to keep everything buried deep inside. It was easier that way.

So nobody knew about the terrible wrench caused by the children's departure, the void they had left. A deep wound inside him that would take months or years to heal. Perhaps it never would. Quite possible.

After the dead mouse episode, he found his slipper under the chest of drawers. He took the tiny corpse by its tail and went outside to chuck it on the muck heap.

And standing there in the middle of the yard in his pyjamas, the seat of his trousers still wet, he asked himself, in all seriousness, how he was going to put it to the little kitten that it would be better, so much better, if it ate what it caught. Such a waste to kill something for no reason. Too much like human beings. What was the point? Not a good idea to imitate, puss.

But how could you explain something like that to a cat?

And a little one at that. Barely four months. What did that make it in human terms – a seven-year-old?

And how did you know it had understood?

No, Ferdinand, was no longer the man he used to be. And hadn't been for some time now. He would have to pull himself together.

By the end of the morning the sky had cleared. He took the opportunity to put in a load of washing.

It was a matter of some urgency. After the same dream three nights running, he no longer had any clean sheets. And no pyjama bottoms either.

And by the way, if one day he had to tell someone what he felt after the children left, he would surely say that once the last suitcase was in the car – a last kiss for the little ones and the door shut – a huge chasm had opened up under his feet, a black hole, deeper than a well. And that turmoil had never left him since. From then on it would become part of his life. He understood that.

But there was little chance he would ever talk about it. It wasn't his style to bare all in front of anyone.

4

FERDINAND IS BORED —
BUT NOT FOR LONG

After lunch he put the washing out to dry. Then he wandered off towards the barn. As he passed the tractor, he couldn't resist jumping in and starting up the engine to see if still worked. Then he went into the workshop. On the workbench he saw the plaque for Alfred: half engraved, it had sat there unfinished for weeks. With a twinge he cast an eye over the tools and mechanically started to sort some old nails. He didn't feel like doing anything, so, not to worry, he went off in the car instead. He slowed as he came to the path leading to Marceline's house, thought about stopping off to ask how she was, but in the end decided to drop by later, perhaps at the end of the day. He went as far as the village. After parking a fair distance from the Place du Marché he took a stick out of the boot and walked up the main road with an exaggerated limp. He didn't meet a soul. That was a bit of a disappointment. Arriving at the café in the square, he ordered a glass of white wine and settled himself at a table outside. He'd made a habit of this for two months now.

The clock on the town hall showed it was three-thirty.

Just an hour to kill before the end of school: the one time he could see his grandchildren, the Lulus. Ludovic, eight, and Lucien, six. He'd give them each a kiss, before Mireille arrived to whisk them away to their new home, using homework as her excuse. All said in a slightly apologetic tone to make it seem more plausible.

Just thinking about it brought a lump to his throat.

He took a sip of wine to make it go away. Then he looked around, but there was nothing to see. He shivered.

In the sky a ray of sunlight was trying to slip between two grey clouds. He closed his eyes and stretched to make the most of the warmth. But it didn't last. There was a sharp tapping on the pavement. Tac, tac, tac. A young woman in a suit and high heels was coming towards him. Unusual round here. He calculated there were seven seconds to go before she reached the terrace . . . six, five . . . he pushed out his stick . . . four, three . . . coming past his chair . . . two, one. Bingo! The girl jumped in the air, twisted her ankle and cried "Ow!" She was about to give a piece of her mind to the bastard who had purposely tripped her up, when her eyes settled on Ferdinand. He managed to assume an expression that was so timid, so perfectly contrite, it made her smile. But she soon recovered herself; on reaching the square, she scowled and shot him a dark look, pointing her finger threateningly. Playing the innocent wasn't going to work with her: she knew all the tricks that old people played. Grandparents, she'd had four of them. And she'd done her fourth-year work experience in an old people's home, so . . . Just at that moment he bowed his head. Muriel was pleased to see he knew what she was really thinking. With a feeling of satisfaction she started to adjust her clothing. She carefully smoothed her skirt, giving special attention to her behind (because to have your skirt creased over your bum is *so* not a good look), she banged her bag several times against her calves to dust it down, tidied up her hair, and without another glance at Ferdinand, set off on her way, suddenly worried she might be late for her meeting (with the bloke from the estate agents, about renting a room, but what could she tell him, she had no deposit, or any of that stuff, oh – my – God).

Ferdinand was happy. He had managed to make a pretty girl smile. That sort of thing didn't happen every day. Well, alright, it hadn't been a very broad smile. And she wasn't such a pretty girl – to be honest she looked a bit tarty, with her high heels, tight skirt and the spare tyre around her waist – but that wasn't important; he had won his smile for the day.

The clock was now showing quarter to four. Only three quarters of an hour till they came out of school. Looking up at the sky he realised that the two grey clouds had merged into a single, ominously dark, mass. He remembered the washing he had put out to dry; he told himself there was still time to go home before it started pissing down. He was going to have to step on it to make it in time.

He was annoyed with himself for having stayed for so long outside the café. His legs were stiff. It took a while to stretch them and when finally he managed to stand up, his son, Roland, appeared. He came and stood right in front of him, with his paunch sticking out.

"What are you doing here?"

"What are you on about? You know I live just opposite."

If Roland had stirred himself to come over, it was bound to mean he had something important to talk about. But as usual his son didn't know how to handle it or where to begin. To gain time he shifted from one foot to the other and cleared his throat. Really irritating.

"So?"

"Well I was just thinking that if you keep on messing around with that stick of yours, you're gonna cause an accident."

Ferdinand sat down again with a sigh, took out his pipe and pouch of tobacco.

"That it?"

"No . . ."

"Well?

"Well, Mireille and I, we can understand it if you don't want to come into the dining room, but we both think it'd be a lot better if you came and had your drink on our terrace. It'd be more normal, don't you think?"

"Sounds like an invitation."

He took his time, drawing a few times on his pipe. To wind him up just that little bit more. Roland hated to see him smoking.

"That's nice of you, son. I appreciate that. Only thing is this white wine, I don't know why, but it's better here. There's no getting away from it."

Roland did not take the bait. Once again he felt a sharp pain in the left side of his ribcage but nothing that could be seen as suspicious or completely abnormal (he had checked it out with Doctor Lubin, who assured him it was just tachycardia). Then after instinctively clearing his throat several times he turned abruptly to go back home. To his own restaurant. On the other side of the square, fifty metres away at the most. With its own terrace for smokers. He took great care to maintain a natural, dignified walk. His head held high, shoulders back, the bottle-opener dangling from the end of a string, beating against his thighs to the rhythm of his step – neat. Except that very soon he felt something awkward. Something seemed to be stuck in the middle of his back, right between the shoulder blades. And it began to seriously get to him. If he had followed his instincts he would have turned round there and then, and gone and punched the idiot's lights out, standing there smirking behind his curtains. Made him swallow that patronising little expression. Christ, it got on his nerves! But he had promised his wife he would keep his cool. Quick. Calm down. Think. Try to . . . In any case, if his rival's old goat of a father had come over for a drink on his terrace, he'd have been wearing the stupid little smile himself. Just to annoy him.

Yes, it was true, now he came to think of it. He felt calmer. Strangely, the thought cheered him up.

But as he was about to enter the restaurant, he caught the expression on his wife's face, at the back of the dining room. Here we go again, feeling very small. No family stuff in public, Roland, we've already discussed it. Yes, but you see, Mireille, P'pa winds me up. He pushed open the door. The bell tinkled. Mireille turned away without saying a word. Anyway, he already knew what she thought. That if old Ferdinand died on the spot, there and then, from a heart attack or, better still, a brain haemorrhage, it would be a great relief.

Roland didn't much like his wife having such thoughts, so he preferred to look elsewhere.

He would sweep the floor. Think about something else.

Meanwhile, Ferdinand, who didn't wish to know how he had provoked his son (and daughter-in-law), was returning to his car. And, on this occasion, forgetting to limp. But he was in a hurry. And at any moment it might rain.

5

MURIEL — LOOKING FOR A ROOM AND A JOB

Another wasted journey. And Muriel wanted to make that idiot estate agent pay for it. Especially since she'd had to skive off college. Not to mention all the effort she'd put into creating the right look, with her suit, tight skirt and high heels. She wasn't used to it. She'd put on a bit of weight so her skirt dug into her waist and her shoes had given her blisters. To cap it all, her left ankle had started to swell up after the old man on the café terrace had tripped her up. It had put her in a very bad mood.

Feeling under attack, the estate agent protested feebly. It's not easy, you know, landlords change their mind at the drop of a hat, so it makes it difficult for us to do the job right. In your case, yes, you're quite right, we should have phoned you to tell you it had gone, but we're snowed under with work, we didn't have time. As he droned on, blah blah, she looked away, it gave her time to calm down and to avoid chucking the particulars in his face. Before leaving she forced herself to smile and shake his hand, and asked him to contact her if anything came up. And just to make sure it sank into his little bird brain, she went over it all once again: a room, furnished or unfurnished, with a shower and toilet, it didn't matter if it wasn't en suite, in the village or nearby, and of course nothing too expensive. It was really urgent: she'd be on the streets if she didn't find anything by the end of the month. He said: I'll do that right away, Mademoiselle, you can rely on me. As she went out she slammed the glazed door hard, but turned quickly as she did so – with wide eyes and her hand across her mouth – as if to say: Whoops! Silly me! Didn't mean that! He acted as though he was used to it: he waved goodbye and gave her a little wink at the same time. It made her want to throw up.

The town hall clock said four o'clock. She had three quarters of an hour before her other important meeting that day. Searching in her bag she found the change she had lost in the lining, so now she could buy a coffee. She went into the Bar de la Place and sat down at the counter. Louise joined her soon afterwards. When they discovered they had both dressed up for the occasion they burst out laughing. At school they had only ever seen each other in jeans and trainers. And now Louise was all made up. Muriel thought it looked a bit slutty, but stopped herself from saying so. Louise was cool; no need to hurt her feelings. They had their coffee and at twenty to five, feeling really stressed, they crossed the square and went into the restaurant.

The boys had just come back from school and were sitting at a table doing their homework and having tea. When the two girls walked in Ludo's jaw dropped mid-mouthful. Their elegant walk, the shape of their gorgeous breasts, the heady perfume and Louise's bright red lips, he'd never seen anything like it. Mireille noticed the effect it was having and gestured to him to get on with his homework. She invited the girls to come and take a seat some distance away and offered them a coffee. They didn't dare say no. But they'd already had five that day, so it looked like there'd be tears, heartburn, the shakes, and insomnia. Particularly for Muriel, who for some time had suffered from all of these. It had got so bad she had thought of giving up drinking coffee altogether and taking up tea. Well, not today anyway.

Mireille asked them a few questions. No, they had never worked in a restaurant before. But they really wanted to. Yes, they were nineteen and both in the second year of their nursing course. They were really enjoying it. Yes, of course, they did have flat shoes. It was much more practical for work and you could walk fast without turning your ankle. Yes, they did need to earn a bit, at the end of the month they often didn't have enough to buy food. It was tough. Mireille left it at that: she told them it was O.K. They looked at each other, unsure whether "O.K." meant they had got the job. But Mireille soon explained how things worked, what they would have to do, the time they would need to start, that it was better not to use perfume as it spoiled the taste of the food, and by then they were no longer in any doubt. True, it was only the one day, but it was exciting nonetheless. In that part of the country there was very little in the way of casual work, except for the harvest or grape picking.

Now, if things worked out, there might be other possibilities. Weddings, stag dos, birthdays, retirement parties, they sometimes had that sort of thing round here.

They shook hands. And with Ludo still watching, starstruck, Muriel and Louise went out of the restaurant. Limping, because new shoes often made you do that, and with high heels it was worse still. They waited till they'd left the main square before taking them off and starting to run barefoot down the road, along the near-frozen pavement, shouting with joy at having found their first job.

6

PARENTS AT WORK,
KIDS ON THEIR BIKES

Saturday.

Mireille had prepared some sandwiches for the kids' lunch. That evening it was the big hunters' dinner. She had taken on four extra staff: Muriel and Louise to do the waitressing and two hands in the kitchen, all of them students. It was cheaper than using qualified staff. The drawback was they'd never worked in catering before, so everything had to be spelt out and that wasted time. The atmosphere was rather tense. Roland bustled about all over the place, barking like a yappy little dog, and losing his temper, something he apparently inherited from his mother. The two lads in the kitchen found him quite a handful, so they took breaks whenever they could. Kim, the sweeter one, explained to the girls that they did this so they wouldn't lose it with him. Muriel and Louise joined them outside for a smoke and a bit of a laugh. They were lucky working in the dining room: it was less stressful there. The owner, Mireille, kept a close eye on them, which was a pain, but she was nice, so it was alright.

Ludo and Little Lu stayed upstairs in the flat the whole morning. They played together, and then did some homework, as Mireille had asked them. About midday they started to feel hungry and they raced downstairs to see who could reach the kitchen first. Ludo won, of course. He was older. Seeing his father labouring at the stove, cheeks on fire and sweat trickling down his neck, Ludo stifled his cries of triumph. And Little Lu, coming down behind him, his bitter complaints. But it was too late. The racket they made had already had an impact. His eyes bulging, Roland turned and yelled: "Get out of here! Don't disturb me!" In a panic they fled, racing out through the main dining room. Mireille managed to stop them. She could see Little Lu was about to cry, but she was in a hurry, so she pretended she hadn't. She handed them their sandwiches, reeling off a list of instructions. First go outside and eat, so you don't make a mess and get crumbs everywhere – careful, for goodness sake! Yes, Papa was a bit stressed, but they must understand that these big dinners always made him like that. There was pressure; he had a lot on. So today, they must be good and manage on their own, just like grown-ups. And the weather was nice; it wasn't raining any more. That was lucky, they should make the most of it and play outside all afternoon. Did they understand? Together they nodded and said: "Yes, Maman." She handed them their coats, opened the door, and told them to go outside, now, please.

They ate their sandwiches on the steps without speaking. Then they had a think about what game to play: Hopscotch,

Tig, or What's the Time, Mr Wolf? But to be honest they weren't that keen on any of them. So they went to fetch their bikes from the garage. They were only allowed to ride them in the backyard behind the restaurant, so it wasn't much fun. Their parents always told them not to go on the road, because they were still too little and cars were dangerous. Ludo agreed that in Little Lu's case that was true. He was still a baby: he'd just started at primary school and only rode a trike. But Ludo was in the third year and had his cool mountain bike, so it was really stupid. All the same they did race round in circles for a quarter of an hour, before they stopped. And started to get seriously bored.

But not for long. It was Ludo who had the idea. He went to look for some string in the garage. He tied one end to the saddlebag on his bike and the other to the handlebars on Little Lu's tricycle. And leaning forward, with one foot on the pedal, he waited for the right moment to go.

Half an hour later they had only managed two kilometres, and they were already tired.

It was alright at the beginning. Little Lu helped Ludo a bit. But after a while he just let himself be pulled along, without pedalling at all. He kept looking behind to keep an eye on the road. It was his job to give the warning when he heard a car coming. He was very conscientious about this. Ludo, of course, was responsible for the traffic ahead. When something came, they quickly parked by the side of the road, laid their bikes in the long grass and hid in the ditch until the car had gone past. They did that to prevent anyone recognising them and telling their parents. But all the stopping took time. Also it was Saturday, market day, and there was quite a lot of traffic.

After the bend Little Lu couldn't see the road any longer, but he still heard something and shouted: "Car coming!" They crouched down in the ditch, craning their necks to watch the vehicle go by. But this time it wasn't a car, it was the lady who sold vegetables and honey at the market. They didn't know anyone else who went round with a donkey cart.

She stopped by them. Berthe, her dog, came over and had a sniff.

"You looking for snails, kids?"

"No, just having a rest."

"That's nice. Where are you off to?"

"To see Ferdinand, our papi."

"He's going to get a bit of a surprise, isn't he? You know you've still got two kilometres to go."

"That's O.K."

"Do you want a ride in the cart?"

Of course they did. She went up to the donkey.

"Now then Cornelius, my dear, will you take these two youngsters to their papi's house?

Little Lu and Ludo laughed with embarrassment. Marceline whispered: "We can't be sure he'll agree, you know." She felt in her pocket and slipped them each a piece of carrot. They held out their hands. The donkey delicately took the bits, and munched them while nodding his head.

"Oh, I'm so glad you said yes. Thank you, Cornelius, my dear."

The children stared at one another, both taken in. They hadn't realised donkeys could understand words so well.

7

THE LULUS AT THE FARM

Ferdinand on the telephone:

"Hello, is that Mireille? Don't suppose you've lost anything today, have you? No, it's not a riddle. Right, I'll explain. Ludovic and Lucien have just turned up at the farm with their bikes. They're fine, I was thinking I'd make them some crêpes for tea."

He held the receiver away from his ear as she gave a shout. Then:

"Yep, that's it, on their bikes . . ."

"My neighbour, Madame Marceline, found them up the road on her way back from market."

"Just a bit tired."

"Of course I've told them off. They've promised me they won't do it again."

"I can bring them back after tea, but . . ."

"These dinners finish late, don't they?"

"One in the morning . . ."

"Two o'clock? You poor things, you're going to be knackered."

"If I were you, I'd . . ."

"But it's natural to be stressed, Mireille. I quite understand."

"You're right, I think it's better too."

"O.K., Mireille."

"Don't worry, we'll manage."

"See you tomorrow then."

"Yes, after lunch."

"Night."

He hung up and, gambolling like lambs, the two boys threw their arms round his neck. Little Chamalo was scared and went off to hide under the bed. It took them ages (and most of the leftover roast chicken) to make him come out.

Ferdinand had to change the menu for supper. Unanimously they voted for spaghetti.

8

LAUGHING UNDER THE DUVET

The children shared the bed in the room next to his. In the past it had been Henriette's room. But Ferdinand had changed everything since then: the bedding, the wallpaper, even the decoration. Roland loved his mother's collection of china ornaments, so Ferdinand gave them to him. In their place he put Ludovic and Lucien's work since they started nursery school: drawings, paintings, pasta necklaces, play-dough sculptures and toilet rolls with Father Christmas heads.

It was much nicer like that.

He left the adjoining door ajar, in case the boys woke during the night.

Worn out by all the cycling, Ludo was the first to go to sleep. Beside him Little Lu still had his eyes wide open. He clutched little Chamalo close to him. Eventually he nudged his brother in the ribs and speaking in what he thought was a whisper, asked:

"You asleep?"

"Mm."

"You know, Ludo, I'm pretty sure I don't love Papa anymore. How about you?"

"Yep, me too."

"That right?"

There was silence and then Ludo went on:

"He's a pillock."

"Is that a swear word?"

"Yeah."

"Oh, right."

Little Lu was delighted.

"What's it mean then?"

"He's an idiot."

"In that case yeah, Papa's a big, fat pillock!"

They dived under the duvet to stifle their laughter. And little Chamalo seized the chance to flee.

From his room Ferdinand had heard every word, but hesitated to intervene.

On the one hand he felt he should. On the other hand . . .

He wasn't supposed to have heard, so he smiled. Told himself that children these days were dead cheeky. He no longer remembered what he had thought at that age – if he could it would be interesting to compare the two. He tried, but nothing came back. Little Chamalo curled up against him and eventually went off to sleep, purring in his ear. Not really what you need when you're trying to think.

9

MIREILLE HAS HAD ENOUGH

The organisers of the dinner had produced a list of guests willing to stay sober. These designated drivers would take their mates or partners home at the end of the evening when they were completely legless. But, as always, there were a few unable to hold out. Two drivers down already. Mireille had spotted them. Almost two in the morning, the evening was far from over and her feet really hurt. She thought about the moment when, due to a shortage of staff, she would have to take them home herself. Not a thrilling prospect. There was always the risk of finding herself with a bloke who, inhibitions gone after all that alcohol, would try and kiss her, grope her breasts with one hand, the other on his flies. Or the sort who'd vomit over the car seats. No she wasn't excited by the idea. She looked at Roland. He didn't excite her much either. Or at all in fact. He'd finished working in the kitchen an hour ago and had sat straight down at one of the tables. He was drinking a lot and laughing loudly. Everything she hated. In her eyes it was common and inappropriate for the owner of a restaurant to mingle with the customers. In fact she found it difficult to stand anything he did. Particularly since he'd put on weight. At first she'd thought it was just a passing phase and she would get over her disgust. But that paunch of his just kept on growing. She'd had a belly like that herself just before she had Ludovic. Or was it Lucien? Both times it was just the same. She hated to see herself so deformed. Not her thing at all. She lost her desire and her libido. For months. And even afterwards, it had never come back like before.

It amazed her that she could still feel so jealous. Reminded her of the days when she was still in love. It had been her idea to take on the lads, not girls, to help Roland in the kitchen. To avoid putting temptation his way. You never knew. There's not much space in a kitchen: you're can't help touching people. It's noisy too, you need to have eye contact, and that's bound to create a bond. Also there's the atmosphere, the heat of the ovens, the teamwork; adrenaline flows. Anything can happen. The head chef going off with the young commis chef at the end of the evening – it's not just in books or in the movies. No wonder she freaked out. The same thing had happened to her, nine years previously. She had been temping one evening in a restaurant where Roland worked.

Mireille knew how these things went. She had tried it herself.

Still, she had no regrets about having taken on the two girls for the waitressing. They were both great. Students at the nursing college. That should teach them to be organised and stay calm in any situation. That wandering hand incident, well done! It had happened to Louise, but Muriel, the cooler one, had gone to sort it out. She stood right in front of the bloke, slapped him one in the face and with a smile asked if the service was satisfactory, and whether there was anything else Monsieur required. The people around him clapped and the evening went off without any further hitches. Ace.

Mireille was bored. She went to the kitchen to check if the two hands had cleared up and were getting on with the dishes. That way there would be less left for her to do on the Sunday morning. She pushed open the door. Kim and Adrien were sitting on crates draining the wine from the customers' glasses. They must have been at it for a while: they were doubled up with laughter. When they caught sight of her they didn't bat an eyelid and asked her to join them. Her first instinct was to give them a piece of her mind. But it was two in the morning. Fifteen hours working non-stop, so . . .

She went back into the dining room, gestured to the girls to join her in the kitchen, took a bottle of champagne from the fridge and popped the cork.

"Come on, it's late and it's raining, I'm going to take you all home. Thank you, you've really put a shift in."

They raised their glasses.

"Chin Chin!"

And the boys found it hilarious to add:

"But not Snowy!"

Alcohol was like that; it made you stupid. At least that's what the three women were thinking. But they hadn't started drinking yet.

10

LEAKY ROOF

The storm began at about two in the morning. Violent winds, sheets of rain. Breathtaking. Inside her little house, Marceline hadn't slept. She spent the night moving furniture, putting buckets and bowls under the leaks and running out to empty them. Exhausting.

Now she was going to inspect the damage in the light of day. She took the ladder from under the hen shelter and dragged it to the house, rested it against the wall, stepped back to check if it was in the right place, then adjusted it several times. Twenty centimetres more to the right, ten to the left, reassuring herself it was stable. All the while floundering in the mud. As she put her foot on the first rung, she told herself that wearing a skirt wasn't very practical. She went back inside, took a pair of trousers from the shelf, only to discover that all her clothes were soaking wet. There was a leak she hadn't spotted, right over the cupboard.

Standing in front of the ladder she hesitated. Humming nervously as she plucked up courage. She climbed one rung, then another, stopped to get her breath back and tried not to look down at the ground. She was still only half way up and already her legs had gone wobbly. She was feeling giddy. She looked up and saw the clouds gathering. Soon it would rain again. She climbed without stopping. Her eyes tight shut. When she reached the top she opened them again and saw the state of the roof.

Cold rain, like stair rods. Marceline had put on her raincoat and stuffed the pockets with all the plastic bags she could find. She went back up the ladder. No hesitation this time. Desperately she tried to seal the gaps between the tiles with rolled-up bags. She knew how feeble these repairs were, but for the moment she had no other solution.

Totally focused on rescuing her house, she didn't hear the dog bark or the children call out:

"Ma-dame! Madame Marceline!"

Ludo and Little Lu shouted as loud as they could. A little further away Ferdinand had stopped to look at the roof and was sadly noting the extent of the damage. The dog came over to him, rubbed against his legs and placed her head under his hand for a pat. Up above, Marceline had run out of plastic bags, so she started to come down. Finally she saw the children at the foot of the ladder, their faces craning up at her, streaming with rain. They laughed and danced in the puddles, two little imps wearing oilskin coats that were far too big for them.

"We've got some carrots for lovely Cornelius and some apples too."

She didn't dare look at Ferdinand. Not so much because

of the vertigo. But to avoid the look of dismay on his face.

Just as well it was now raining even harder, she decided. No-one would see her tears or hear her sobs.

Under his shelter Cornelius took the carrots and apples offered by the children and ate them while nodding his head.

"Are you pleased to see us, Cornelius? You do like carrots, don't you? And apples too? Can we have another ride in the cart sometime?"

Little Lu was so proud. He could prove to Ferdinand that the donkey understood everything.

"See! You thought we were making it up."

Ludo nodded and gave the two old people a knowing look. It was like with Father Christmas. He was pretending, for the sake of his little brother. That was the privilege of being the older one. Or the disadvantage.

Ferdinand helped Marceline put a tarpaulin over the roof. When they'd finished he told her she needed to phone the roofer and ask him to come immediately. She looked away. He didn't insist. After a while he added that if in the meantime she wanted to store her things at his place, that wouldn't be a problem. She thought it over, went into the house, and came out again a few minutes later, carrying something bulky in her arms, swaddled in a blanket. Holding it like a baby, she laid the delicate object in the back of the car. The children were curious. A cello, she told them. It was fragile and didn't like the damp. If it stayed under the leaks for too long it could catch a cold just like a human being. So she asked them to look after her cello while the work on her house was completed.

11

IN WHICH FERDINAND BRINGS BACK THE CHILDREN

In the car Little Lu asked in a whisper why she was so sad, the lady with the donkey. Ludo told him it was because of the storm: the roof of her house was so rotten it had flown away. And now, Madame Marceline was going to die of cold, no doubt about it.

They both remained silent for the rest of the journey.

Once they arrived at the farm they went round the empty rooms trying to find the best place to put the musical instrument. They had understood their instructions well. Not too close to the heat, but not too far away either. As they looked the children asked Ferdinand why he didn't invite Marceline to come and live with him. The house was big, there was plenty of room and the roof didn't leak like at her place. He laughed and replied that they didn't know each other well enough to suggest such a thing. But why? He explained that generally you only shared your house with members of your family, not usually with strangers. Why? Because you didn't feel quite right in other people's houses, you didn't have the same tastes or habits. Why? At that he just said: Because, that's the way it is. Ludo grumbled: That's not an answer. And Ferdinand agreed with him, but he had no other arguments to offer, so he preferred to leave it at that. It seemed he had more pressing things to do than think about such trifles.

Finally they found the perfect place. They put the swaddled instrument on a table. Then they raised the blanket to look underneath, but there was a case and they didn't dare open that. Next time they would ask Madame Marceline to play the fat violin for them, Little Lu said. The other two smiled.

After lunch Ferdinand took the children home.

When they arrived at the restaurant Mireille was busy cleaning the kitchen floor. She shouted at them to keep off the parts she had washed. They had to wait for her to finish before they could give her a kiss. She warned them that Roland was still asleep, so they couldn't go up to play in their room yet. This irritated Ferdinand but he gave nothing away, just muttering between his teeth: What a bloody idiot! Mireille acted as if she hadn't heard and offered him a coffee. He looked outside. The wind had started to blow again and it was raining horribly. He refused, saying he was in a hurry. He gave Ludo and Little Lu a kiss and left.

As soon as the door was closed, Mireille turned to Ludo.

"You and me need to talk."

All that going on the road with their bikes and giving Little Lu a tow, he'd known he'd pay for it, sooner or later. It was only to be expected, it had been his idea and he was the oldest. But before she had time to get going he asked, innocently:

"By the way, Maman, will there be another big dinner next week?"

"No, why?"

"Just wondered."

Little Lu made no attempt to hide his disappointment.

"Sugar! That's rubbish."

Which annoyed Mireille even more. So Ludo got a right earful.

12

LUDO PREFERS TO GET AN EARFUL FROM MIREILLE

So, even if she does go on a bit and sometimes says nasty things – she's quite strict, my mother – I still think it's better when she has a go at us, not Papa. He always wants to slap us, or smack us. I hate his face when he gets worked up and his eyes look like they're about to pop out. He goes bright red just like that and his voice goes all high, like a lady shouting. When he loses it you have to make sure you're by the door, then you can get away if he lifts his arm. He never runs upstairs after us, especially now he's got so fat. He gets tired out and he starts snorting like a bull. One of these days I reckon he's going to die of a heart attack. Anyway if he did try to catch us, Maman would definitely stop him. He doesn't dare lift a finger against her. He's too scared she'll leave and never come back. But he says his mother was right about bringing up children. She was called Henriette, his mother. Weird sort of a name. Mamam, she tells him she hates people who hit their kids. She thinks it's horrible, reminds her of her parents. They used to hit her all the time when she was little. And one day the police came to get her and they took her away to live with Uncle

Guy and Auntie Gaby. They were nice to her. They didn't have any children, so they spoiled her a lot. She tells everyone they're her real parents, but it's not true.

When it's Maman who has a go at us, it's easy. You just pretend you agree with everything she says, even if it goes on for hours and in the end you have to cry real tears, jump into her arms, say you understand and you'll never do it again. Then that's it, it's all over. And afterwards sometimes you get to have a glass of Coke and a packet of crisps before supper. Once Little Lu managed to get some choc ices as well. She was really angry with Papa and she screamed it was all his fault she'd had kids, and because of that her breasts were all horrible and spoilt. If she'd stayed single she wouldn't have had any kids and she'd still be pretty. Little Lu was standing outside the door. He heard everything and started to cry like a baby. When she saw him she cried too, even louder than him. And then she took him in her arms and said it wasn't true. She didn't really mean what she'd said; it was just to wind up Papa.

Maybe. But, I think she's right about her breasts. They do droop a bit.

Anyway that time me and Little Lu got to have choc ices. And to be honest, I love that.

13

FERDINAND IS PLAGUED
BY DOUBTS

Ferdinand passed the track leading to Marceline's house. He slowed down, but didn't stop. He told himself she might take it badly, all these visits one after the other. She might think he wanted to interfere. And he wasn't like that. So he went home. It was pelting down and he didn't feel like doing much, except sit by the stove and have a glass of mulled wine. He thought about switching on the telly but first he had a look at what was on and that put him off. Nothing but tedious soaps, he'd have to find something else to occupy him. He went upstairs. Seeing the toys on the floor and the unmade bed where the children had slept, he felt a twinge of sadness. At that very moment they were bound to be getting an earful from their mother. That was O.K., just so long as she wasn't too hard on them. It was the most he could hope for. He tidied up and made the bed. Then he started to look for little Chamalo, but couldn't find him anywhere. The kitten must have gone out for a stroll. As it was tipping down, there was no chance of it coming back in a hurry. That cat didn't like water.

Going back downstairs he did a detour via the room where

they had put the cello. He lifted the blanket in which it was wrapped but, like the children earlier, didn't dare open the case to look inside.

Finally, on reaching the kitchen, he stood there aimlessly.

The damage caused by the storm at his neighbour's house, the holes in the roof, the leaks in the ceiling, and the cold and damp which had enveloped her house . . . It made him shudder just to think about it. He tried hard to get on with something else: listen to the radio, do the crossword, thumb through a catalogue. But he kept going back to it. If he started to work out the answer to a clue, invariably he would raise his eyes to the ceiling and see the leaks again. Listening to the radio was even worse. All they talked about was the record rainfall for the time of year and the plunging temperatures.

So he immersed himself in his D.I.Y. catalogue. His favourite pages, the last ones, were reserved for inventions. The kind that gets entered for the *Lépine* competition, but a little less glamorous. A pan for sweeping up crumbs, a telescopic pole for taking down jars from a high shelf, a left-handed vegetable peeler or a gadget to pull up your socks without bending down. He quite fancied the scrub-free magic sponge that cleaned everything from floor to ceiling, all for a very modest sum. But he was afraid he might be disappointed. Better to carry on dreaming that it would work. Carefully complete the order form and never send it off. And so, once again, that was what he did.

At the end of the day he heated up the remains of the

spaghetti from the day before, watched the news on the telly and after channel flicking for a while, found a Western. But for once he didn't enjoy it. The girl was beautiful, but after three days riding through the desert, pursued by baddies, with nothing to eat or drink and no chance to wash, she still looked like she'd just stepped out of the salon, with her make-up immaculate and barely a crumple in her clothes. Usually that didn't bother him, but right now it was all too much.

He switched off the telly and watched the rain outside.

The cat had not returned. He felt alone and depressed, so he went to bed.

But he didn't sleep.

His mind was in turmoil and his emotions all mixed up. Sadness, shame, anger, guilt . . . He was annoyed with himself, hated his coldness and lack of humanity, came up with excuses, but wasn't convinced. So even after the cat came back and despite the purring in his ear that usually had a strong soporific effect, he got to thinking. Asked himself all those questions: if, where, what, how, not to mention why. The answers seemed obvious. But it was all too easy, so the doubts returned. Worn out by all this toing and froing, he came up with a solution: the following day he would ask his best friends, Guy and Gaby, what they thought. That would be more sensible. Just as he was about to doze off in the usual way, he asked himself what his late wife Henriette would have made of it all. And at that point it suddenly became clear to him. Five-thirty in the morning. He still had quite a lot to do and a load of feelings to unpick.

But above all he had to put the finishing touches to his idea. Without disturbing Chamalo he got up, made himself a coffee and let his mind wander, waiting for it to be a reasonable hour to visit.

14

FERDINAND REHEARSES HIS LINES

Standing outside Marceline's front door, Ferdinand didn't dare knock. He kept going over in his head what he was going to say. Finding the proper tone, the right words, it was tricky. So . . . Hello, Madame Marceline, it's me again. Ferdinand. I've come back to say that I've been thinking all night about it, I've gone over things again and again, I've weighed it up, dissected it, racked my brains and I'll be straight with you: you can't stay in this house any longer. In the state it's in, it's dangerous. The beams are rotten; the roof could collapse at any moment. You have to leave. Urgently. As you know, since my kids left I've been living on my own at the farm next door. For nearly two months now. I've got several rooms not being used, with separate entrances. All mod cons. Not so long ago we were three families living there, you know. Three generations. Without treading on each other's toes. So, there you are, it couldn't be easier. You can move in today, stay till the work's been done, for the winter, and some of the spring, of course. Then if you want there's room in the stable for your donkey and a henhouse for your chickens. And . . .

He knocked.

The dog barked and from inside, Marceline's voice, barely audible, told him to come in.

She was sitting on a chair, shaking and looking dazed, with her cat in a ball on her knees, its fur all matted.

"He's come back. I think he's hurt."

"Do you want me to take a look?"

"Yes, please."

Ferdinand felt the cat. The dog anxiously tried to stop him, slipping her muzzle under his hand to move it away, whining, begging him to stop. He gave her a pat. And in a reassuring tone said that nothing seemed to be broken, but it must be quite a bruiser this tomcat, it had scabs all over. No need to worry though, in two to three days he would be right as rain. Cats were thick-skinned. Marceline sighed and bit her lips to stop herself from crying.

A pause. Then Ferdinand helped her out of her chair and put her raincoat over her shoulders.

"Come on, Madame Marceline, you can't stay here."

He took the cat in his arms, and went out of the house first, with her following. The dog followed too.

15

THE INVITATION

Marceline was asleep in the armchair, her cat curled up on her knees and the dog at her feet. They were no longer trembling. Ferdinand took the opportunity to go back to her little house to save those things that could be damaged by the water and cover the rest with tarpaulins. When he returned Marceline was still sleeping. He hung the clothes from her wardrobe out to dry. Then he set off again with the dog, this time to feed the donkey and the hens.

Night fell. He went home, added some wood to the stove, and put the soup on to heat. Little Chamalo burst in, thinking it was dinnertime. Coming face to face with the dog, it stopped dead: with hair on end, and pupils dilated, it arched its back; sprang up, spitting like one possessed, and raced off to hide. After a while overcome by curiosity it came back to see the new arrivals. The old tomcat was asleep. No danger from there for the time being. The dog on the other hand was watching it, her tail wagging and her ears down. What was that supposed to mean? When the cat did that it was because it was angry. But the dog seemed content, even wanting to play. It was the first time the cat had come across a dog.

No wonder it wasn't sure how to handle things.

Ferdinand left them to get on with it. He went to fetch a bottle of wine from the cellar, laid the table and nibbled at a crust of bread to stave off the pangs of hunger. The soup was still warming on the corner of the stove. As he went by he lifted the lid to see how it was doing. He had a taste. Too thick, so he added some water. He gave it a stir. He looked at the time. Marceline and her cat had been sleeping in the same position for more than three hours. The situation was starting to become worrying. He went over and bent down to listen to their breathing. She was snoring very gently, as was the cat. He felt reassured. At that exact second she opened her eyes, saw him leaning over her and cried out. Ferdinand and the tomcat jumped, the dog barked, the kitten fled.

She looked around her, completely disorientated.

"What's happened? I can't remember."

"The storm? The roof?"

"Has it collapsed?"

"No, no, just leaks. But they're big ones."

She got up, the old cat in her arms.

"Cornelius!"

"I've given him something to eat. And your hens too. Everything's fine."

"Are you sure . . . ?"

"Yes."

He poured out some soup, invited her to sit down and put the bowl in front of her. He offered her a glass of wine. She didn't dare refuse. After two swigs the colour returned to her cheeks and she almost managed a smile. They talked of this and that – nothing in particular. She found it more restful not to think too much at present.

At the end of the meal she thanked him for all his help. So kind and thoughtful of him to feed her donkey and hens while she was asleep. And now this invitation to supper. She was feeling much better, but it was late and really she had to get back. She got up, put on her raincoat, and gathered her things, which he had hung out to dry a little while before. Ferdinand was desolate. He had been hoping he could make her understand his idea without the need to talk about it. But it was no use. He would have to spell it out, now, find the right words. To gain time he asked her if she wanted to look round the house before she left. She agreed out of politeness. They went through the rooms, left empty since his son and family had moved out. Then they went upstairs. He was still searching for inspiration. Finally he launched into a woolly and convoluted preamble where he talked of an idea, which was not entirely his own, because in fact, it was funny, it had been the children who had thought of it first – by now he was well away – in short since her house was no longer habitable and there was room here, it seemed only natural to suggest, and of course he would be delighted if she agreed, for her to come and stay. They're so logical, my little Lulus, don't you think? As it happens, this is the room where you'll sleep tonight. The bed's all made up. You just need to lie down. Tomorrow you'll feel more rested and you can have a quiet think about what you want to do. Good night, Madame Marceline. Oh yes, one last thing. Do you like tea or coffee in the morning?

"Tea."

"That's lucky, I've got some."

As he went out he patted the dog's head and shut the door behind him. He was pleased. He'd managed to say everything and seemed to have been convincing. It hadn't been so difficult after all. Well, he'd see what she decided the next day.

She remained motionless a long while, with her raincoat still over her shoulders, the cat in her arms and the dog at her feet. It was as though her brain had short-circuited.

"But . . . well alright, good night then."

16

TEA FOR BREAKFAST

"Two teaspoons? O.K. And once I've poured out the boiling water, how long do I leave it for? How do you mean, it depends? Five minutes for a reasonably strong brew? Alright, alright. Thanks for the advice. And Gaby, has she got over her flu then? . . . Oh shit . . . But . . . I didn't know. Mireille didn't say anything. Would you like me to have a word with her about it? Alright. You poor sod. Tell me, if you need anything, be sure to give me a ring, O.K.? Do you hear, Guy? Ring me. Even if it's in the middle of the night. That's what friends are for. Give her a big kiss from me. I'll drop in and see you soon. You'd prefer tomorrow? O.K., Guy. See you tomorrow, mate."

Ferdinand looked at the clock. It was seven and not yet light. He rummaged through the dresser and eventually found what he was looking for: a large teapot and a cup with matching saucer. Henriette had won them in a lottery. Or perhaps in a shooting competition. She tried them all. She must have been after the big prize again: the pressure cooker. But she'd won the tea service instead. It had never been used: she didn't like tea. She had her coffee with chicory. He rinsed the cup under the tap, wiped it, put it on the table by the gold metal tea caddy. It was alright, didn't look too bad at all.

The kettle started to whistle.

He poured the water gradually into the coffee filter. He thought back to the conversation and Gaby's news. So sudden. Christ almighty, it made you feel sick. And Guy would be left on his own. Would he be able to bear it? They had been inseparable. And now, wham . . . Try as he might Ferdinand couldn't think of any other couples that much in love. He was moved by the thought. Not that he was jealous. He wouldn't have been able to stand being tied down like that. He was just touched that it could happen.

His train of thought was disturbed by a stampede on the stairs. Berthe came in and rubbed herself against his legs, tail wagging and tongue hanging out, followed closely by little Chamalo. Ferdinand picked him up in one hand and held him close, and with the other patted the dog's head. They seemed to be getting on. So far so good.

He put the teapot down in front of Marceline, and helped himself to a bowl of coffee. They drank together in silence. Finally he asked how her night had been. Very good, thank you. And the old tomcat was better? He'd been sleeping since yesterday, but hadn't eaten a thing. Recuperating, as you'd expect. As long as that was it. Had she begun to think about . . . ? A bit. He paused for a while. She was in no rush to let him know. He told himself he must let her choose her moment, so he asked another question. She knew Gabrielle, didn't she? Who?

Guy's wife. A couple of old farmers like himself. Gaby, yes, of course, they were friends, they always went to the library together, but it had been a fortnight since . . . Well, she wouldn't be able to go there any more. Why was that? She's on her way out. She wasn't sure what he meant. She's got a one-way ticket. Did that mean . . . ? Yes, she hasn't got long. Oh.

"I'm going to see her tomorrow. Would you . . . ?"

"Yes, please."

"She'd like that."

17

MARCELINE DOESN'T UNDERSTAND

After breakfast, Marceline put on her boots and raincoat and set off with the dog. They were both in a hurry to get home. They could hear Cornelius braying in the distance. As they arrived at the small track leading to the farmyard, he trotted up to them. As usual he had managed to open the gate to his pen and had gone round the vegetable garden in search of something to eat. But finding nothing he returned to the yard, complaining noisily. Marceline stroked him for a long time, whispering sweet nothings in his ear. And she also scolded him just a little, as she'd noticed that during his walk he had trampled all over the cabbages. Then she went down to her house and slowly pushed open the door. The tarpaulin on the roof had given way. Half torn off, it was flapping against the wall in the wind. Five centimetres of water covered the floor. Dismal.

An hour later it started to rain again.

Ferdinand was washing up the breakfast dishes. He heard a bark, so he went to open the door. Berthe splattered him from head to toe, as she carefully shook her coat on the doorstep. She was happy to see him, rubbing herself against his leg. She ended up completely soaking him and when she had been patted enough she ran to lie down in front of the stove.

Marceline crossed the yard, clutching two large vases. The wind had beaten back her hood, her hair was soaked, and the water trickled down her face.

She stood in front of him, and looked him straight between the eyes.

"You know very well I don't have any money to pay rent."

"I haven't asked you for anything."

"So why the offer?"

"It's natural."

"What's natural?"

"To help each other out."

"I don't understand. We've hardly said a word, let alone shaken hands. You barely knew I existed and now all of a sudden you're offering . . ."

"I know. But don't you worry about that for now, Madame Marceline. Come on in."

He held back the door to let her through. She hesitated, then finally went in. He wanted to help her. But she brushed him aside, and holding the vases tightly, ran upstairs.

When she came down again there was a faint smile on her face, as though she wanted to apologise. He told her not to worry, it didn't matter, we all have our little foibles. And she replied that one day – but not just now because at the moment she was so on edge she would definitely cry – she would explain why she preferred to carry the vases herself. In just a few words. It wouldn't take long.

18

MOVING OUT, MOVING IN

Ferdinand had attached the trailer to the tractor and Marceline harnessed the donkey to her cart. In less than an hour they had loaded up all her belongings. The biggest problem was the wardrobe. They rested it on one side, and slid it as far as the door, but there it got stuck. Ferdinand pushed and he pulled, he huffed and he puffed with all his might, but nothing doing. After a while Marceline began to laugh. He worried she might be about to break down. But soon he understood it was the situation that amused her. He was amazed. To be able to laugh after all she'd been through was simply astonishing. Well, it astonished him anyhow. He resumed pushing the wardrobe. It wouldn't budge. In the end Marceline decided she might as well leave it there. It was not worth breaking their backs for such a short time. She didn't have that many things. She could live without it.

Returning to the farm, they piled her belongings in the room the kids had chosen for her cello. It was a small, bright room, on the ground floor, not far from the kitchen. Not at all like her house.

She chose that room because of the window looking out

on Cornelius's stable. It would reassure him to see her, and she could keep an eye on him. No sooner had he arrived than he started to examine the bolt on the door of his stall. It wouldn't take him long to work out how to open it. Two or three days at the most. And then what would he get up to once he was out? This was a donkey that liked to go where he pleased, visit the surrounding area, particularly the vegetable garden. Ferdinand might not be too keen on finding hoof marks in the middle of his vegetables. Only she could see the funny side. And even then, not always.

She finished sorting her belongings. A noise made her turn and she jumped. With his nostrils pressed against the windowpane, Cornelius was watching her with a baleful eye.

There was nothing for it: if she wanted any privacy she would have to put some curtains over the window.

19

GUY AND GABY

Guy was brushing Gaby's hair. So fine and so delicate, he was afraid of damaging it. He scarcely touched it, just enough to make her look neat and tidy. Then he asked her whether she wanted it fixing with a hair slide. She did. He looked for his favourite, the one with the large white flower. Was it a camellia? She grumbled that she'd told him a thousand times it was a gardenia, but he could never remember. There, she was ready. He smiled at her. She could see from his eyes that he thought she was beautiful. Since her return, he no longer brought her the mirror. Each time she asked for it he came over all vague and told her he'd lost it. She thought he had broken it and didn't want to own up. Lying, just like a little boy afraid of a telling-off. A white lie. Nothing too serious. Well, enough. As for the mirror she wouldn't mind being told it was in smithereens, on the contrary. For some time now she no longer liked looking at herself. Water must have got inside, or the back had got warped, in any case, she couldn't recognise her own reflection. In Guy's eyes at least she was still his Gaby. Unlike this cheap mirror, he didn't judge things by appearances. He sought her out in the depths of her being and illuminated her with his love.

With him at her side she knew she wouldn't be afraid when her time came.

Guy got out some little cakes and made some tea and coffee for the guests.

He and Ferdinand went out into the garden for a stroll and to smoke a pipe, while Marceline gave Gaby's legs a massage. It did her good. She had been bedridden for a fortnight. She could no longer feel her blood circulating. Now it was coming back, she felt less cold. She wanted to talk. She asked Marceline to come close, so she wouldn't have to strain her voice. She was very thin and exhausted, her breathing was laboured, but there was still a slight twinkle in her eye. She asked after Cornelius – what had that donkey been up to, to make her smile? Marceline told her how he had learned to open the bolt on the pen, and described his walk round the vegetable garden and the trampled cabbages: her punishment for having left him alone all night. He was a cheeky one, that donkey. Her smile faded. So you see, Marceline dear, I'm on my way out. Yes, Gaby, I know. I didn't think it would happen so soon. There are things I miss already. Like what? I'd have liked to live through another spring, with the buds on the trees, the hawthorn, and the smell of lilac, and the sound of the bees gathering pollen. And what else? I'd also like to hear you play the cello. Oh Gaby, please . . . You remember that C.D. you once played me? It was so beautiful, that music. But Gaby, you know I can't. Never mind. It's just I'd have liked it so much. Go on, go and get

Ferdinand quick, right now. Otherwise I'll be too tired to talk to him.

Ferdinand came and sat down by the bed.

Still beautifully turned out, my Gaby. With your hair slide and your camellia. She grumbled that it was a gardenia. Oh yes, it's strange; I can never remember that name.

She signalled to Ferdinand to bend down closer so she could whisper in his ear. She told him that when she was gone he would need to keep an eye on Guy. It might be hard for him at first without her. He would need reminding of the things he had to do, his responsibilities. Mireille and the two little ones would need him. She was afraid he would forget. And then if ever Guy wanted to join her, he should tell him that they would have all the time in the world to be together. All eternity, perhaps. She looked at Ferdinand, hoping for a response. He was moved and kissed her on the forehead. Of course he would tell Guy that. And if her man didn't behave, he'd give him a kick up the arse. She could count on him. Gaby smiled and closed her eyes, worn out from having talked for so long. That was good, now she could sleep peacefully.

20

GABY SMELLS OF VIOLETS

When Mireille found out about Gaby, she wanted to have her admitted to hospital again. Someone must have made a mistake, got the files mixed up. It was just a bad case of flu at the beginning, wasn't it? Why would no-one listen to her? Then she realised it was not a mistake. Gaby really was going to die. She felt betrayed. For the second time in her life, a mother was going to abandon her; she was not going to be able to forgive that. For two days she didn't come to see her. On the third day, Guy went to fetch her. They cried a lot. Eventually they looked at one another and hugged each other. They shared the same suffering. Together they would find a way of facing up to it.

The next day Marceline phoned to say she would drop by late in the morning. Gaby was already very weak, but she asked Guy to prepare her especially for the occasion. She had chosen her black dress, the one with the lace around the neck. Then she wanted her hair done. He brushed her hair lightly and put on a hair slide so it would stay in place. The one with the gardenia. Finally she asked for a drop of perfume in her ear. The one that smelled of violets, a little touch of spring. There, she was ready. And Marceline arrived. Opening the cello case, her hands started to shake. She sat down by the bed and closed her eyes before starting to play. By the time she raised the bow, the shaking had stopped. It was that piece from the C.D. And, hearing it live, Gaby found it even more beautiful. When it was over she put her hands together, but hadn't the strength to clap. She gestured for her to come close and kissed her on the cheek. Marceline thanked her. Gaby protested: "I'm the one who should be saying thank you. It's the first time I've ever had someone perform a concert for me. And gosh I'd have hated to miss something like that."

And huddled up against one another, they burst out laughing like schoolgirls. Marceline whispered: "Perhaps in the place where you're going you'll meet my daughters."

"Yes, I'll give them a kiss for you, I promise."

Three days later Gaby died. Guy was at her side. He held her hand and she was not afraid.

21

LUDO'S LETTER
(WITHOUT THE SPELLING MISTAKES)

Dear Auntie Gaby,

I hope you're well and it's warmer where you are than it is here. There was a frost last night and Uncle Guy had to bring in your lemon tree, otherwise it would have definitely died outside. You see the sort of weather we're having. It's winter now.

I'm writing this letter because there are things I want to tell you and I didn't have time before.

I broke the lamp with the merry-go-round, the one you gave me for my birthday. But I didn't do it on purpose. It was too near the edge of the table and the wire caught my foot. Afterwards Papa wanted to slap me, like he normally does, but Maman stopped him. I've really had it with Papa, you know. I'm wondering when they're going to get divorced. Maman's annoyed with him all the time and one time she even called him a sad bastard. I know I shouldn't tell you that, because she is really a bit like your daughter and you could be sad to know she uses swear words. But if you ever think you brought her up badly, I swear it's not true, you did a good job. You mustn't worry. And also, really you shouldn't care, because swear words they don't mean anything. Me, I use them all the time and I know they don't mean anything. I liked the ones you used. It was funny when you got cross and said damn. Little Lu often says damn and sugar, like Ferdinand. He's only little so it's O.K.; it's not stupid. In my class we use real swear words, like shit or pissed off. But we're older, that's why.

Before when you were still here, Maman wasn't so scared of everything. Now she always wants us to stay with her all the time and if you fall over or get a cold, she starts thinking we're going to die too. It's a real pain. I hope it's not going to carry on like that.

Uncle Guy is sad but he's trying not to let it show when we go and see him at his house. He wants us to think it's all normal. Sometimes he tries to tell jokes, but they're not funny, so we don't always laugh. Maman, too, she acts like she's alright. Except one time I heard her crying in the night. It's normal to cry when you haven't got a girlfriend or a mother anymore. It would make me cry anyway if I didn't have mine. But I wouldn't mind if it was Papa.

So Auntie Gaby, that's all I've got to say.

If you ever want to write back or tell me something, it would be good if you could come back in my dreams. I'll try and remember when I wake up in the morning.

Big kiss.

Ludovic – your darling great-nephew who loves you loads.

Little Lu wants me to write that he sends kisses too. I've seen the drawing he's done for you – it's of a butterfly. Also you'll see his signature is really rubbish.

Lucien

22

SIMONE AND HORTENSE WAITING

Eleven o'clock.

Simone and Hortense had been waiting for an hour, sitting on their chairs right by the door. Knitting.

That morning they had got up earlier than usual. Simone began by adding some wood to the stove. Next she put on the coffee pot, to heat up the coffee from the day before. Then, shuffling along in her old slippers, she went back to the bedroom to join Hortense and together they fetched their things from the wardrobe: black dresses, knitted jackets of speckled wool, woollen stockings that had gone at the knees, fur-lined ankle boots and winter coats with the imitation astrakhan collars. It was a long time since all these things had seen the air. They smelled of mothballs. Hortense asked herself how long it had been, but before she had time to finish Simone had already replied on her behalf.

"One year. Since Alfred's death."

"Alfred? What did he do then?"

"He was a smith of course, just think, Hortense!"

At that moment in the kitchen the coffee started to boil and Simone rushed to take the pot off the stove, pursued by

Hortense shrieking, boil the coffee, spoil the coffee! Naturally she was irritated. But, boiled or not, they drank it. It wasn't nice and they had nothing to sweeten it with. The sugar had got left off their last shopping list. It was like that with Hortense: she had her memory lapses.

On the windowsill a cat with a half-torn ear and gammy leg started to meow pathetically. Simone let her in and then raised her voice so the neighbours could hear.

"You hungry, you poor thing? Alright, come on in, we'll give you a drop of milk. Shame!"

Shutting the window again, she carried on muttering:

"They'd let the creature starve, that lot. I tell you they've got hearts of stone."

They gave the cat a large bowl of milk, and then both sat down to watch it lapping. The cat took its time, licking its whiskers and wiping its chin. It was just about to jump up on Simone's knees to be stroked, as it did every morning, when she leaped to her feet, brushed it away and opened the window again.

"Out you go, shoo! You can come back tomorrow for your cuddle. Really! The little bastard will end up making us late. For Christ's sake, Hortense, it's nine o'clock. We'd better get cracking."

And she rushed off to shut herself in the loo. Hortense glanced at her list pinned up by the dresser. Nine o'clock: do the budgies. Nine-ten: have a wash. Just as she'd thought. So she opened the cage, changed the water and hung up a new stick of millet. She watched the birds pecking away.

It was then she had her little bad patch.

Out of the corner of her eye she could see that it was already ten past nine on the clock. She remembered clearly that she had something to do. What made it worse, she knew what it was. But then, just like that, nothing. She no longer wanted to move, didn't want a thing. Just to stay where she was and watch the birds. And that's what she did. But after a while she told herself that when Simone came back from having done a number two, she would not be well pleased. She needed to pull herself together, collect her thoughts. So she quickly closed her eyes and retraced her steps in her head, like a top sportsman before a race. Ten past nine: have a wash. Open the cupboard under the sink, and get out the two bowls, take the flannels and the ladle, get hot water from the large pan on the stove, without spilling any, fill Simone's bowl, the red one, and then hers, the blue one, pick up the flannel, rub it with soap, start with the face and the neck, then under the arms, and between the legs.

But it didn't do the trick. She started to panic.

At that moment Simone came out of the loo and noticed something was wrong. Gently she went up to Hortense, took her by the hand and talked to her almost in a whisper. Just like she'd have done with a sleepwalker.

"Don't worry, Hortense. Look at me. See, I'm not angry. Anyway, what difference does it make if we've had a wash? No-one will notice. It'll be a secret between the two of us. You'll see:

we're going to have a good time. When people come up and kiss us, we mustn't look at each other, do you understand? Otherwise I won't be able to stop laughing. And so what! If you stink a bit, you just have to put on a bit more cologne than usual, that's all."

Hortense chuckled.

They got dressed and splashed on some perfume, emitting little cries. Then they sat down on their chairs opposite the front door, and took out their needles and balls of wool.

It was now eleven o'clock. They had been knitting for more than an hour, while they waited for someone to come and fetch them.

Hortense dozed off. She couldn't remember much about where they were supposed to be going that day, but she trusted Simone. Her brain was not full of holes. She didn't need to make notes; she remembered everything. Hortense would be lost if they weren't together. Completely lost.

23

LATER, AT GUY'S HOUSE

Roland took care of the buffet. He didn't want anything too elaborate, but he did want it to be comforting. It was cold, real autumnal weather. So he went for a big vegetable soup and put some pasta letters in the children's. He thought they might like that. Then he made some meat pasties and little potato cakes. They were nice and filling. Also practical, you could eat them with your fingers. And there'd be less washing up.

He reheated the mulled wine. It was going down well, hardly any left.

Everyone's cheeks were flushed, they were bright-eyed and talking loudly. But it wasn't just the wine. The majority of those present were old and not quite all there. That didn't help.

In the corner Mireille was chatting with Marceline.

It was the first time they had exchanged more than a few words. But things were different now. Marceline and Gaby had been friends, so that was definitely a bond between them. Mireille thanked Marceline for having played the cello for her auntie. It had been very pleasant and soothing. She hadn't known before that she was a musician. How could she? She'd always seen her with her cart and donkey, selling fruit and veg at the market. Marceline explained that if she had played the other day, it was because Gaby had asked her, she couldn't say no. But she hadn't done so for a long time. Not for years, in fact. Mireille didn't dare ask why; must be something serious. It could wait for another time or until they knew each other better. In the meantime she said that she would love it if Ludovic and Lucien, her two Lulus, could learn an instrument. She really needed to do something about that.

Ferdinand, Raymond and Marcel accompanied Guy into the garden. The four of them sat on the bench, staring ahead without saying a word.

But not for long. Mélie and Mine joined them, in a state of high anxiety.

"We've forgotten the Lumière sisters!"

The four men leaped to their feet.

"Oh shit!"

They raced through the house, put on their jackets, went out into the street and stopped by Ferdinand's car, which was parked nearby. Guy took the keys. He was the only one of the four to have drunk just the one glass of wine. He set off. The other three followed on foot.

The house was barely fifty metres away. When they arrived, they hesitated, embarrassed, trying to work out what their excuses could be. But before they had time to knock the door opened. It was Hortense, who had at that very moment come to her senses.

"We thought the funeral was this morning. Can you imagine? Sometimes I think we're not quite right in the head!"

The four men bent down to kiss them and Simone started to chuckle. Hortense glared at her, but that didn't work, it only made her laugh even more.

Hortense was embarrassed and pushed her towards the door.

"Get in the car, Simone!"

And then a little more discreetly:

"Stop messing around. What on earth are they going to think? I'm ashamed of you."

24

VISITING GUY

Ferdinand. The days following the funeral.

Ferdinand went round to see Guy, turning up unexpectedly at his house. If he didn't answer, Ferdinand would go round and enter by the kitchen, as that door was always open. He had noticed Guy was starting to let himself go, forgetting to eat and wash, and even, on some days, get out of bed. The only times he made an effort was when Mireille dropped in with the children on Wednesdays and Saturdays. On those days he got dressed, tidied up, and opened the shutters. But the rest of the time he could just sit there, doing nothing. For days on end. It was clear he no longer had an appetite for anything.

Ferdinand was worried. He tried to think of reasons to make Guy go out. He suggested going to the café to see people, say hello to friends, or play a round of dominoes. But Guy wasn't interested. Apart from Mireille and the children, the one thing that stirred him from his lethargy was talking about Gaby. Only then did he become animated. He needed to remember, to say the words. The idea that he might forget something about her threw him into a panic. Ferdinand listened. He knew Guy would need time to get used to living without her. It could take months or years. Perhaps the wounds would never heal. Quite possible. One thing was certain: he wouldn't neglect him. He had given his word. Besides, it would never occur to him to drop a friend.

Marceline. Saturday, after market.

After stacking her crates in the cart, Marceline went to see Guy. She knocked at the door, but there was no answer. No sound from the house, nothing. She went round via the garden and tapped on the window, as she used to do when she came to fetch Gaby to go to the library. Pressing against the pane she could make out a silhouette. Guy was sitting motionless at the kitchen table, staring straight ahead. She opened the door and went in to sit down beside him. Patiently she waited for him to turn and look at her. His eyes were sunk deep in their sockets, as though looking inwards. His voice barely audible.

"Nothing makes sense any more."

He wasn't ashamed to say that to Marceline, she knew how he felt. Gaby had once told him about the sadness in her life.

She stroked the back of his hand. Talked in a low voice:

"I think she'd have wanted you to keep on trying."

He didn't want to cry in front of her. Quickly he got up and left the kitchen.

"Would you mind putting on some water to boil, Marceline? I'll only be a minute. Will you stay and have a cup of tea?"

*

Mireille. Sunday evening.

The children were in bed, but it was still early and she didn't feel sleepy. She decided to sweep behind the bar. Roland had already gone up to bed. She heard him talking on the telephone, saying: "Hi, Daddy." Crazy at his age. She was angry with him. About that and everything else. But particularly for not understanding how difficult she found it being on her own right now. Sod the medication, she was going to help herself to a small glass of sherry. She gulped it down. Looked at the time again. Eight-thirty. That was O.K.

She arrived at Guy and Gaby's front door. One more thing to get used to. From now on she would have to think of it as just being Guy's house. She was all at sea.

The shutters were closed and no light filtered through. She knocked. No reply. She went round the house, through the garden, and tapped on the kitchen window. Still no answer. She pushed the handle and the door opened. She called out. No response. She switched on the light and saw the chaos: washing-up piled high in the sink, the remains of a meal on the table, dirty clothes strewn across the floor. She had never seen the house in such a state. She ran upstairs, flung open the bedroom door, saw Guy, fully dressed, stretched out on the bed, and gave a shout. Startled he turned towards her.

"I didn't hear you come in. What is it, Mireille? Why are you shouting?"

No real reason. She just needed to see him; that was all. She was worried because he never answered the phone and then seeing all the mess had shaken her a bit. That was why she had come upstairs. And when she discovered him there, lying on the bed, she really thought he was dead. They went down to the kitchen. She needed a drink. He offered her a sherry. She went for water instead, because of the medication. She drank it in one. That was better. She hugged him tenderly, told him not to worry: everything would be alright. She was going home. The next morning she would come back and help him tidy everything up.

25

ROLAND ON THE PHONE

"Hi P'pa."

"Is that you Roland?"

"Course it is. Who else calls you Papa?"

"It could have been Lionel phoning from Australia."

"When's the last time he did that?"

"I dunno, last Christmas, maybe. So, why are you ringing?"

"No reason. It's been a few days since I saw you hanging round the terrace of the café opposite, tripping up young ladies with your stick, so I wondered . . . is everything alright?"

"Yeah, yeah, everything's O.K."

"Not too bored on your own?"

"Nope, not at all."

"You found something to occupy yourself?"

"I've got loads of stuff to do."

"That's good."

"How about you? How's the restaurant?"

"Alright."

"And the kids?"

"O.K."

"And Mireille?"

"She's gone back to work. It helps take her mind off things. Doctor Lubin has prescribed some antidepressants, you know."

"Lubin? He's not in gaol yet then?"

"Every time . . . Maybe we should avoid the subject."

"You're right. Anyway, nice of you to ring."

"It's nothing, P'pa."

"No, it's nice of you. Look, Roland, you do realise your sons are six and eight and they call me Ferdinand. Don't you think . . . ?"

"Hang on a minute, what's the problem? Does it embarrass you if I call you Papa, is that it?"

"No, but at forty-five, you'd think . . ."

"What's age got to do with it? Anyway, it's too late. I can't call you anything else. I don't believe it. I ring you to find out your news and what do I get? A kick in the teeth. Always on the attack, eh? I'm totally wiped out, you know. It's eight-thirty in the evening and I'm off to bed. Right, bye P'p—Oh shit, I'll never get it right."

"It's not a problem, Roland. Night, son."

Ferdinand went back and sat down at the kitchen table.

That evening it was Marceline's turn to make supper.

She used only produce from her garden. Honey from her bees and eggs from the hens. She explained she couldn't face killing the animals she had reared; she always grew so attached to them. She had solved the problem by not eating meat any-more and that worked very well. Naturally he didn't ask too many questions, but he understood she didn't have the money.

Because three days earlier when he had cooked chicken, she had eaten it and had even complimented him on the taste.

He had learned the odd little thing about her apart from that. She was Polish and not Russian or Hungarian, as he had thought. Her first name was Marcelina, but everyone called her Marceline. She had got married here about twenty years before. That was why she spoke French so well, with hardly a trace of an accent. She had worked in many foreign countries while she was a musician. He really wanted to know why she wasn't doing that any more, but didn't dare ask. Must be a pretty good reason. But not worth pursuing now.

She put the dish on the table. He winced.

"You don't like swedes?"

"I do, but they don't agree with me."

"I've put a bit of baking soda in."

"How come?"

"It stops the side effects; you don't get windy."

"You really think that works?"

"It makes a difference. You'll see."

"I hope so."

She was amused.

"Well, if not, we'll take our coffee outside after dinner. Then you'll be more relaxed. Let's hope it doesn't rain again!"

Ferdinand thought of Henriette. They had never joked together in that way.

After dinner they went outside. Not because of the swedes – the baking soda did seem to work – but because Cornelius was noisily demanding a bit of attention. That donkey had a mind of its own; he liked to come and go as he pleased: he'd leave his stall and wander round the farm, spending a long time working out how to get through gates and fences, particularly ones leading to the vegetable garden. But when evening came he wanted you to go and say good night to him before he went to bed. Just like a child.

26

MIREILLE HAS SOMETHING TO ASK

When Mireille arrived in the farmyard, the kitchen light was still on. She was surprised to be greeted by barking. Velcro, Ferdinand's idiotic dog, had died at least six months earlier and he'd sworn he would never have another. He must have changed his mind and forgotten to tell them. Irritating. But she soon got over it. There was something she wanted to ask. She told herself that after all the poor guy was entitled to his little ways. And besides, it wasn't so stupid to have a dog when you were lonely.

She got out of the car, the dog recognised her and came over wagging its tail. Mireille was puzzled.

Ferdinand came to the door. He was surprised to see her. It was the first time she'd been to the farm since moving out. Almost two and a half months now. And at this time of night, with no warning. He was anxious. Roland had telephoned an hour before, but hadn't said anything. Had something happened to the children? She shook her head. No, everything was alright. She looked worn out and slumped into a chair. Marceline offered her some coffee. Or a tisane perhaps? She wanted something a bit stronger. If there was any wine left, that would be nice. Marceline went to find some of her celebrated plum wine, while Ferdinand got out three glasses. They drank a toast. Then wishing to give them a bit of space, Marceline excused herself, saying she must go and see to her old cat.

As soon as she had left the room Mireille looked at Ferdinand with a flicker of a smile. He sensed she was going to say something stupid, so he preferred to take the initiative and explain why Marceline was there: the storm, the leaks in the roof, the danger it might collapse . . . He'd decided to invite her to his house, it was large, and had been empty since they'd moved out. He added that at first of course she had refused, but he'd managed to convince her, so she was going to stay until the work on her house had been done. Mireille remained silent for a while. Finally she muttered, as if to herself, that she hadn't seen it coming. It had been such a long time . . . She had thought she knew her bloke's father: an old guy, a bit cold, rather stiff, not that nice, and yet now . . .

"So is that all you came to tell me, Mireille?"

"No, I wanted to . . . But hang on a sec. First, I want to know why you haven't told anyone all this."

"So people won't get the wrong end of the stick. You know how sometimes they get daft ideas."

"That's true."

She helped herself to another glass.

So, two sherries, an antidepressant tablet, and a couple of glasses of plum wine later, she started to explain the reason for her visit.

Her Uncle Guy wasn't well. Ferdinand must have noticed he was letting himself go. In just a few days he'd lost so much weight, it was awful. And those dark lines round the eyes, his expression. The children no longer wanted to see him: they were scared. He was like a ghost.

She started to cry, but carried on talking.

So perhaps if he wasn't on his own, he might get his appetite back? He could do stuff; look after the children, and her too. She needed that, particularly at the moment. Maybe it would work better if he no longer lived alone.

Ferdinand patted her hand. She snuggled up to him. It was the first time they had been so close. He wasn't used to it. He searched in his pocket and offered her a hanky. She blew noisily into it and waited for his response.

"He's as stubborn as a mule, your uncle. If he doesn't want to do something, you'll have a job making him change his mind."

"But it might work if you suggested it."

She waited for him to agree.

"I'll go and see him tomorrow."

The combined effects of the alcohol and medication finally kicked in. She was in no fit state to drive. Ferdinand took the keys off her, put Marceline's bike in the boot (his own tyres were flat) and took her home.

Fortunately, it didn't rain on the way back. But it was a long time since he'd been on a bike, so he had to stop several times for a rest.

He knew he'd pay for it the following day.

27

AN OINTMENT

And sure enough he did. When Ferdinand woke his legs were stiff and painful and his backside had been mangled to a pulp. It was bad so that he couldn't stand up or sit down. At seven-thirty he finally called Marceline to help. She brought him a bottle of homemade ointment. It worked for her; he should try it. He was sceptical, but had little choice. He rubbed some on in the way she indicated and felt a little better. He managed to get down to the kitchen without too much difficulty and he congratulated her on the miracle cure. He was careful not to refer to a "home cure". The poor thing had just lost her home and he didn't want to upset her.

While drinking their tea and coffee, they talked about the previous day. She found it touching that Mireille had dropped in unannounced to see him. Especially as it was the first time she had done that, if she'd understood correctly. She had looked like a little girl – so distressed and so vulnerable. Ferdinand pulled a face. He had known Mireille for some time. And even though she gave the impression of being sweet and all that, you couldn't trust her too much, not our Mireille. She wasn't like that all the time. She could be very strict, for example with her own children. And with him she had done everything possible to stop him seeing them, on the grounds he used too many swear words. Whereas, in fact he was very careful about that. But yes, granted, it was true she had seemed vulnerable the previous evening. And he was very touched that she had come round for a chat.

They tried to imagine how they would arrange things if the three of them were to live together. They did a tour of the house.

There was really no reason not to.

They said goodbye and each of them left.

Marceline was behind with her vegetable garden. She needed to make the most of the dry weather to plant the garlic and winter shallots; sow some broad beans and peas. Before the ground became too hard with the frost.

28

GUY LOSES FIFTEEN KILOS

Guy didn't come to the door. Ferdinand went round by the garden, but the kitchen door was locked. He had to break a window to get in.

Now they were sitting side by side on the bed. Ferdinand talked of Guy's responsibilities for Mireille and the children. Gaby wouldn't have liked his letting himself go in this way. It would have made her really sad. But above all, for God's sake, she'd have hated the fact that he had gone a fortnight without a shower or shave. She would have certainly demanded a divorce: the bloke stank! Guy gave a weak smile.

Down below Mireille was doing the washing up. She broke a glass and shouted: oh shit! Ferdinand raised his eyebrows, but secretly he was delighted.

Guy agreed to have a wash. He could barely stand, so Ferdinand helped him up. It wasn't surprising, he'd lost fifteen kilos in a fortnight and was skinny to begin with. He fetched some clean clothes from the wardrobe and leaned on Ferdinand's arm to go down the corridor. On reaching the bathroom, Guy pushed him away and told him to go downstairs and wait for him. He could wash himself; he wasn't bedridden.

An hour later, he came downstairs looking neat and clean-shaven. Mireille had prepared something for him to eat: scrambled eggs, with tea and bread and butter. He made an effort, but had trouble getting it down.

At a quarter past ten Mireille had to go out to work. She gave Guy a hug and rubbed his back, as though trying to warm him up. He whispered in her ear not to worry, he would soon be better. She stepped back to take a look at him and he smiled. She wanted to believe him and gave him an affectionate kiss. She had opened the door to go out, but then changed her mind and came back to kiss Ferdinand on both cheeks. Until that point she had always kept her grumpy father-in-law at a distance when she greeted him.

Once they were alone together, the gloves were off, Ferdinand went on the attack. He asked Guy what he would miss most if he ever had to leave his house. And Guy snapped back: nothing. Ferdinand was caught off guard; he hadn't expected such a blunt response. So Guy explained. Neither he nor Gaby had ever really liked the house. On retiring they had been forced to sell the farm to pay off some debts and with the money left over they hadn't been able to find anything better. That's how it was.

Ferdinand put his cards on the table. He told Guy about the idea that he, Mireille and Marceline had come up with. And of course Guy said no. But Ferdinand was undeterred. He had already found the right words and arguments the first time round with Marceline; he wasn't afraid to start all over again.

He knew Guy like the back of his hand. A right stubborn old git. You couldn't push him; if you wanted him to budge, you had to catch him by surprise.

That's what he tried to do all day, but without success.

Finally, running short of arguments, he put his jacket over his shoulders and said, "You can't stay here, Guy. It's not good for you. Come on, let's go."

29

TWO PLUS ONE AT THE FARM

Guy refused to take any of his belongings, even his pyjamas.
Ferdinand thought that was good. No reason to take
offence. It meant there was still life in the old dog. In any case
he had some pyjamas; he could borrow his. It was weird: since
Marceline moved in he hadn't had the dream, the one where he
swam with the dolphins in the warm, blue waters of a tropical
lagoon. In a way he was sorry, it had been a really nice dream.
But on the other hand he was no longer wetting the bed, and
that wasn't so bad.

When they entered the farmyard Cornelius was standing
in front of the kitchen door, busy examining the handle. A
few minutes more and it was clear he would have opened it.
Guy had of course heard all about his exploits from Gaby – he
could still recall her pleasure, saying how that donkey, he
was one of a kind! But he'd never had a chance to see him in
action. For Ferdinand it was different. He had been treated to
the carrot trampling episode and other unpleasant incidents,
so at first he was not impressed. But he soon melted when
he saw Guy's expression. For that smile alone he would have
gladly invited the donkey to come in, sit down on the sofa

and have a drink with them. One of a kind, that donkey!

They went upstairs and Ferdinand told Guy to make himself at home in Henriette's old room while he reached his decision. The bed was comfortable and the room had been completely redecorated with the children's work. That was where the two little scamps had slept the other night after their bike escapade.

Ferdinand made some soup for supper, with leeks, carrots and pearl barley. At nightfall he heard a scratching at the door and went to open it. The dog made a fuss of him, then went over to Guy to be patted. As though it had always been that way. Marceline came in, having taken off her boots, worn out by her long day in the garden. All she wanted was to get changed, have some hot soup, and go straight to bed. On seeing Guy her expression lit up and she went over to give him a kiss. Ferdinand had succeeded. As she went by she looked at him with a twinkle in her eye and tilted her head, as a way of discreetly congratulating him. But when she went into her room she changed her mind and came back to kiss him on both cheeks. Something she had never done before. All the more surprising since they still addressed each other as *vous*.

After dinner the three of them went out to say good night to Cornelius.

Before she left, Marceline whispered sweet nothings in the donkey's ear and asked him to go easy on the locks, latches and other bolts. Because, Cornelius dear, Ferdinand doesn't get the joke. She stepped back to see the donkey's reaction and he nodded. She was surprised. Perhaps he really did understand everything.

As she came inside an envelope fell from her pocket. Guy picked it up and handed it to her. She had taken it out of the letterbox during the day and forgotten to open it. There was too much to do; it had slipped her mind. She opened the letter with some trepidation. It was the quote for the repairs on her roof. She examined the estimate carefully and when she came to the total (materials, labour, inclusive of tax), she collapsed on her chair. Guy and Ferdinand noticed she had gone pale. She apologised, and said she was so tired, her legs felt like lead, she would have to go straight to bed. They wished her good night, she gave the dog a pat and left.

Guy and Ferdinand were not tired. Flicking through the programmes on T.V., Ferdinand saw there was a documentary about whales due to start in less than five minutes. No way could he miss that. They took two glasses and the bottle of plum wine and rushed into the living room. Like two old rascals, full of mischief.

30

FLU PERHAPS

On his first night, Guy slept rather well. Two spells of ninety minutes. Nothing abnormal about that: he was an insomniac. At about three in the morning he went out for a stroll. He needed to stretch his legs, get some fresh air and a feel for the area. The dog accompanied him to Marceline's house and by the light of his torch he examined the state of the roof. It would cost some to repair all that, he thought. No wonder the poor woman was worried.

Going back, he wandered around the barn. As he passed the tractor he couldn't resist climbing up on it. But he didn't start the engine, so as not to wake anyone. After that he went to the workshop and cast an eye over the tools. He was looking for something to do, but found nothing. Feeling a wave of depression looming, he went back to bed before it overwhelmed him.

Eight o'clock.

Marceline was not yet up. Usually by seven she was already making breakfast. The dog trotted anxiously back and forth between the kitchen and her bedroom door. Ferdinand watched dejectedly. He put on some water to make tea, heard a noise in the corridor and went to investigate. It was Mo-je scratching at the door. He opened it and the old cat raced through his legs. Little Chamalo, who had been waiting for this, ran after him to play but the older cat turned and gave him a clawing to keep him quiet. Best not to annoy him in the morning. There was important work to be done, strolling round the estate; finding good hunting spots; sharpening claws on tree trunks; and marking out new territory. He liked to play, but only when there was nothing else to do. Little Chamalo soon recovered and hurled himself at the dog's tail, as it wagged up and down. Now that was fun.

Nine o'clock.

Marceline still hadn't emerged from her room, and Ferdinand wondered what he should do. He went past the door several times, stopped to listen, but couldn't hear anything moving.

He said nothing to Guy, in case it made him anxious.

At ten o'clock he decided to knock on the door. He thought he heard a groan. He knocked again. Another groan. He opened the door and called out. In the semi-darkness he saw her lying stretched out on the bed. He went over and asked if there was anything wrong. She replied in a shaky voice that she didn't feel well. She had a high temperature, and pains in her legs and back. She thought it was flu. He put his hand on her forehead. She was boiling hot.

Ferdinand went to see Guy in his room and told him what was happening. Guy didn't take it well. It had been just the same with Gaby; they had all thought it was flu at the beginning. Even Doctor Lubin had diagnosed that. Ferdinand asked him not to mention the man's name again. He was useless and a complete idiot. They waited, not knowing what to do about Marceline.

They heard Mireille's car arrive. She had been dying to know how things were going at the farm, but didn't dare phone. She acted as though she had just dropped in to see them, for no real reason, well, just to say hello. Oh, by the way, she had stopped off on her way to pick up a few things from her uncle's house. In case he needed them. His washbag, clean trousers, woolly socks and wellies. You never knew. It often rained. And then there were also some photos lying on the dresser. All this, of course, said in a matter-of-fact tone. Photos of Gaby and the children. She looked at them before handing them over and then burst into tears.

Without even discussing the matter, they decided not to say anything to her about Marceline. She was still too fragile. It was not worth upsetting her with more talk about illness.

So when, a little while later, she asked them about the neighbour – how she was and where she was – they replied in unison that she was fine and had gone out early to work in the garden.

As soon as Mireille had left, Guy sat down at Marceline's bedside, made her take an aspirin, and mopped her brow with a damp cloth. Meanwhile Ferdinand was on the phone to Raymond. He was a healer; he would know what was needed. Raymond replied that he knew how to treat eczema, warts, rheumatism and lots of other things, but not flu. He would pass him over to Mine, his wife. She would be sure to know. Mine did indeed have some remedies – thyme tisanes, brews and poultices, and hot toddies to make you sweat – but she thought that if Marceline had a high temperature it would be better to call the doctor. But please, Ferdinand, not Doctor Lubin! That suited him just fine. She recommended Mélie's son-in-law, Gérard. He was nice, and competent too. Also, he generally came quickly.

31

THE DIAGNOSIS

Gérard called in at the end of the day. He examined Marceline and asked a few questions about her medical history.
She replied that she had never had any health problems in
the seven years she had lived there. Although that was possible,
he suspected another reason. More and more he came across
people who couldn't afford medical costs, and were not covered
by social security, insurance, or any kind of benefit. And, in fact,
when it came to completing the paperwork, she told him there
was no point. She indicated the metal cake tin on the shelf
and told him to take the money due. He replied that they would
see about that later, once she was back on her feet.

Gérard joined Ferdinand and Guy in the kitchen. They
gave him a glass of plum wine, which he enjoyed. And they
waited for his diagnosis.

It was indeed a case of flu. With a very high temperature.
No need to panic for the time being. There wasn't a great deal
to be done, apart from wait and keep an eye on things. Take
her temperature regularly. Make her drink lots of water. And
broth, too. How about thyme tisanes? That would be fine, if
they wanted. Had Mélie suggested that? He knew it. She was

right, though. It was very good. If Marceline had headaches or her temperature went up, they should give her some aspirin or paracetamol. If there was no improvement in three days, they should call him and he would come and review the situation.

As he left he turned to Guy and told him that he had heard about his wife. He said he was very sorry and asked how he had been. Guy replied that he would rather not talk about it for the time being. Gérard didn't press him. They shook hands and he left.

Ferdinand went off to buy what was needed from the chemists. He took the opportunity to do some shopping and before going back he stopped off at Mine and Raymond's to borrow a thermometer. He couldn't find his own.

Now Guy and Ferdinand took turns at Marceline's bedside.

Guy had chosen to do nights. It made sense with his insomnia. Ferdinand would take care of the days. They had to take her temperature every two hours and record it on a sheet of paper to make a graph, like they did in hospital. They also made a note of everything they had given her to drink. Guy had decided that. Ferdinand didn't want to call into question the purpose of such a list. We all have our little ways, he told himself. It wouldn't do any harm.

It was the first time they had used a digital thermometer. Mine had explained how it worked. A few seconds in the earhole and like magic it rang and the temperature was displayed. Like in a science fiction film. Or "Star Trek". They remembered

Mister Spock with his pointy ears, giving injections without a syringe, or a general anaesthetic simply by pressing two fingers on the neck. And woh! People collapsed, just like that, rigid on the ground . . .

And what about teletransportation?

They should get a move on, inventing that. So the two of them could have a go before they popped their clogs.

"Can you imagine it, Ferdinand?"

"Can I just? Beam me up, Scotty!"

32

A THERAPEUTIC THREAT

Marceline had a raging temperature. She seized Ferdinand by the arm and begged him to listen. With bright eyes, she talked about her dog, her old cat and her donkey. There was no-one to look after them. If he would agree to do that it would be such a relief and she would feel so much calmer. Ferdinand's immediate reaction was, of course, to say yes. But then a doubt crept into his mind. What if this became the excuse for her to pack it all in? So he said no. And explained his reasons. The dog? O.K. she was nice enough, but to be honest he preferred it before when she wasn't there. The house had been cleaner and tidier, without all those paw marks and hairs everywhere. Also, she scratched the doors, and that damaged the paint. It looked terrible; he would have to do another coat in the spring. The old cat? It reminded him of his oldest son. It didn't like anyone and was totally self-centred: going out hunting, scratching tree trunks, marking out its territory and giving little Chamalo the odd clout. Not his kind of cat at all. And the donkey? Well, he wasn't amused by him. Animals that had a mind of their own, refused to be shut in, and broke down their gates – they weren't his thing at all. Given all the damage he'd caused trampling in the vegetable garden and all the other places he'd put his great hooves, that donkey was a real pain. I'm sorry, Marceline, but don't rely on me to look after your animals. And if you do ever decide to leave them to me, I'm warning you I won't hesitate to get rid of them. I may seem nice, but I'm not really.

He emerged from the bedroom exhausted. Guy watched him come into the kitchen and slowly got up, convinced there was bad news coming. But Ferdinand said nothing. He took a bottle of wine from the larder, poured himself a glass, drank it in one and collapsed on his chair. The dog went over and rubbed herself against his legs. He stroked her affectionately. Guy sat down again.

Ferdinand started asking questions.

Of course Guy didn't have all the answers, he only knew one or two things Gaby had told him. So he was able to say that . . .

Yes, Marceline had a heavy burden to bear, but he didn't feel he had the right to speak on her behalf.

Yes, she probably didn't have any family. In any case, she certainly didn't have any here.

The animals had definitely helped her to keep going. It was a good idea to threaten to get rid of them; she was bound to react to that.

No, that was enough for now. He wouldn't say any more.

33

THYME TISANE

She tried to run, but something stopped her, shackled her legs, she shouted for them to let her go, not hold her back, otherwise it would be too late, she wouldn't be able to join them, that couldn't happen, she couldn't stay any longer, it was impossible, she cried, she begged, she kicked, but she felt her strength going, she could barely move now, she had no strength left, nothing, not even her voice, it was surely the end. Suddenly she felt calm, her body no longer suffering, it seemed light as a feather, around her the mist lifted, a bit further away she glimpsed her daughters on the other bank gesturing to her, they seemed serene, she smiled at them, finally she was going to join them . . .

"Marceline . . . Marceline . . ."

Guy's voice, gently calling her. She didn't move. He kept trying.

"Wake up, Marceline. Time for your tisane."

She opened her eyes. He helped her up, propped her against the pillows.

"I had a really strange dream."

"You're telling me! It was like you were running and

struggling against something, but in the end you must have got where you wanted, because you seemed happy and calm. A crazy sort of dream."

He handed her the bowl of thyme tisane.

"Drink it before it gets cold."

She did as she was told.

"Olenka and Danuta – are those your daughters' names?"

She nodded.

"You called out their names just now while you were asleep."

"Yes, I remember."

Her temperature fell and Marceline was finally able to get up. Her legs felt all wobbly; she had been in bed for four days. Ferdinand and Guy helped her to the window. She could see Cornelius. He had managed to get out of his stall all on his own and was walking round the yard. Hearing the tapping on the windowpanes, he turned his head and came over at a gentle trot.

34

GUY'S DECISION

Guy eventually decided to put himself in the room that had belonged to Lionel, Ferdinand's older son. He had left thirty years before, at the age of seventeen. There was no chance of him coming back and wanting it now. A strange customer, Lionel. From time to time he would phone with news. Generally at about four in the morning. Down there in Australia it was eight at night but he would forget about the time difference. Or maybe he didn't give a damn. That was probably it; he was a bit like that. Even as a child he didn't have friends: he liked to tear the wings off flies, make his mother cry and convince his little brother he was a vampire. And then he had gone off, thousands of miles away, so he would see no-one and have no ties. He must have found what he was looking for. No wife, no partner, no child. Living all on his own, in the middle of nowhere. And he'd found the work to go with it. Maintaining the dingo fence – the longest such fence in the world. More than 5,600 kilometres. It helps to stop the wild dogs (or dingoes) from attacking the sheep. But it's not very effective, apparently. At least that's what Lionel said and he should know. Given all the time he's spent repairing it.

In order to fetch Guy's furniture they attached the trailer to the tractor and got out a tarpaulin in case it rained. Guy did the driving and Ferdinand sat up beside him on the mudguard. The sound of the engine, the cold feel of the metal seats, the harsh jolting, the smell of diesel, it took them back a few years. During the journey they didn't say a single word. They were too busy relishing those sensations once more.

The move was soon over. Guy only really wanted to take the lemon tree and some tools from his workshop. But Ferdinand insisted, so he decided to take the bed and bedside table, Gaby's dressing table and a chest of drawers in which to store his things. The rest he left behind.

When they arrived at the village square he turned off the engine and told Ferdinand he'd buy him a drink. In the restaurant the bell tinkled and Roland put his head round the kitchen door. He was really surprised to see them. He shouted upstairs:

"Mireille! Come quick, Uncle Guy and P'p— my father are here!"

She ran down the stairs.

The four of them sat down and had a glass of white wine together. Mireille was so happy. She immediately noticed Guy's cheerful expression. In no time at all he had put some weight back on. Clearly the farm air and life in the *ménage à trois* were doing him a power of good. It was then that Roland realised no-one had thought to tell him about all these changes. Annoyed, he got up, trying to hide the pain in the left side of his ribcage; it was psychosomatic, Doctor Lubin had told him, no reason to panic. He pleaded kitchen duties and left the three of them there, talking. That was handy; there was something Guy wanted to discuss with Mireille. It was nearly the end of school, so Ferdinand offered to go and fetch the kids. She agreed – that was a first – and he rushed out.

Meanwhile Guy explained to Mireille that he wanted to leave his house to her.

It didn't hold many memories for him because the real ones, the ones that mattered, the ones of her between the ages of four to eighteen, were back there on the farm. It was already ten years since they had left. So there it was, he wasn't that attached to the house, she could do what she wanted with it. Sell it or rent it, as she pleased. But Mireille wasn't pleased. She gave him a piece of her mind. She thought he was moving too fast, he should think about things before giving it up. And above all take time to see how it worked, living together under the same roof. It had been barely ten days. It was impossible to anticipate all the problems there might be with Ferdinand and Marceline. They might end up getting on his nerves, and then what would he do if he no longer had anywhere to go? He must be reasonable. There were times when she too felt like giving up. Nine years she'd been married to Roland. But she didn't want to make a rash decision and then regret it afterwards. Wanting to separate from husbands or friends, in the end it was a bit the same. In both cases you risked being left high and dry. He needed to have a serious think about it before going down that road.

Guy remained silent.

After a while he handed her the keys. She hesitated and he put them down on the table. He was quite certain he wanted to give that house to her. It wasn't much, but it would be hers and no-one else's. Also Gaby would have wanted that. It had been their joint plan. He didn't need to say a single word. Mireille understood and nodded. Only then did he speak about his own plans. He told her he couldn't carry on living on his own. Two weeks had been enough. He needed to have people around him, share experiences, feel useful. Otherwise he would lose his appetite and the will to live. So that was it, he'd made up his mind. He was going to stay with his friends. The farm was big: he could be independent and have space to himself when he needed it. He had set himself up with a workshop in part of the barn and at night when he had insomnia he did his D.I.Y. there. It suited him very well. Also having several grandparents together in one house wouldn't be so bad for the children. And . . .

Mireille took the house keys, bent down to give him a kiss and whispered in his ear:

"Thank you, Uncle."

35

SWEETS, CHEWING GUM AND
LANGUES DE CHAT BISCUITS

When Little Lu and Ludo saw Ferdinand waiting behind the school railings, they hurled themselves at him, and flung their arms round his neck. Then they demanded something to eat. He didn't argue and they did a rapid detour via the boulangerie. With Mireille they normally went straight home; this time they wanted to take maximum advantage. They chose everything that she forbade: pains au chocolat, chewing gum and sweets. During the journey home they managed to wolf these down and ask all sorts of questions, without, needless to say, leaving room for any answers. They wanted to know if little Chamalo had grown and if he still chased mice, and when could they go to Ferdinand's house? Soon it would be the Christmas holidays, did he know what presents they were getting, and that their parents were going to get divorced soon? There was a pause and Ludo felt he should add something, so he took the gum from his mouth to explain. With the satisfied smile of someone who knows something that other people don't, he said it wasn't definite, of course, but there was a good chance of it happening since Mireille and Roland were now arguing every day. Having finished the sentence he put the enormous lump of gum back in his mouth and started chewing pensively once more and Ferdinand just said: Oh, right.

A little further on he pointed out the Lumière sisters' old shop, and the house where they lived. Of course Little Lu wanted to know why they were called that and also why they didn't stop and say hello, as they knew them and they were cousins, weren't they? Ferdinand raised his eyes skywards, a bit exasperated by all these questions. Without further explanation he went to the house and knocked. No reply. Pressing his ear to the door he heard whispering inside. To reassure the two old ladies he called out his name. Simone appeared, then turned back inside and said: It's alright, Hortense. You can put the gun away, it's Ferdinand and the kids, they've come round to say hello.

They went in and the two old ladies both went into raptures over the children: they were so good-looking and how had they grown, gosh how time flew! It was only a fortnight since they'd last seen them after Gaby's funeral, but neither of them could remember that. Then Hortense invited them to follow her to the larder, her eyes shining in greedy antici- pation as she took out a large biscuit tin, while in a low voice Ferdinand had a go at Simone about the shotgun. The children were no longer hungry, but Hortense insisted they tried several different biscuits. Go on, don't be shy, have as many as you like. They won't keep. The boys politely each took two. Ludo bit into his *langue de chat*, but immediately spat it out again as it was off. He nudged his brother in the ribs, to warn him. But Little Lu didn't understand and cried, ow! and then tried to hit him back. Ludo ducked and managed to whisper that the biscuits were all rotted and Little Lu soon calmed down. Hortense went back to chat with the others, so the boys took advantage. They went over to the budgie cage and discreetly got rid of the old biscuits by slipping them through the bars.

On their way back to the restaurant they saw Guy, sitting with his back to them, talking to their mother. They hung back. The last time they had gone to his house, they had been really scared. He was the spitting image of the undertaker in *Lucky Luke*. And he really stank. Since Gaby had died he didn't seem to want to wash. Perhaps not even his feet! Mireille had explained that was quite normal; sometimes it happened that people let themselves go when they were unhappy. After a while it would pass. But now he seemed his usual self. Neat, clean-shaven, content. They ended up throwing themselves at him and smothering him with kisses. Mireille smiled and looked at the time. Five o'clock. It was a three minute journey from school to the restaurant. They had been half an hour. Ferdinand said he was sorry it had taken them so long; they had stopped to say hello to the Lumière sisters. He also pointed out to Guy that they should be leaving soon. It wasn't a good idea to drive the tractor at night.

He went into the kitchen to say goodbye to Roland.

"We're off . . ."

"O.K."

"Are you O.K. then?"

"Yep, I'm alright."

"And the restaurant?"

"It's fine."

"And the kids?"

"No problem."

"And Mireille?"

"She's fine."

"Oh good."

He hesitated.

"It'd be nice if you all came over and had lunch one day."

"Yeah, why not?"

"How about Sunday?"

"Check with Mireille."

"OK then . . . see you soon?"

"Yeah, see you soon, P'pa."

Roland bit his lip.

"It doesn't matter, son. I don't really mind what you call me."

36

THE LUMIÈRE SISTERS
IN A BLUE FUNK

Ferdinand wiped the table with a sponge before laying it. Then he went to fetch some wine from the cellar. Marceline put more wood in the stove and swept up the bits of bark that had fallen on the floor, while Guy prepared supper. It was his turn. He had decided to cook spaghetti, his great speciality. It was also Ferdinand's, so there was rivalry in the air. Inevitably they asked Marceline to decide between them. But she didn't like the fact it was becoming more and more like a competition, so she refused.

Perhaps it was because there were three of them, they each separately concluded.

In the meantime, Guy's spaghetti with garlic and dried ceps was sheer perfection. Ferdinand would have his work cut out.

At the end of the meal they put on their coats, scarves and hats and went outside to say good night to Cornelius. Then they sat on the bench by the wall, the one with the little awning above. It was supposed to protect against showers, but didn't work too well. That night all was peaceful; it wasn't raining. The two old codgers sipped their coffee and smoked their pipes, while Marceline had a tisane. Her stomach was still feeling a bit delicate from the flu. After a while Ferdinand decided to tell them about his visit to the Lumière sisters. At first he talked calmly, but then became more and more worked up. He described their fear of opening the door, the shotgun brought down from the attic and Simone's shiftiness when he questioned her. Why the shotgun? What were they planning to do with it? Who or what were they afraid of? It was surely only natural to ask these things?

Marceline and Guy both nodded.

And then, he continued, Simone had suddenly decided to reveal all. She had explained that Hortense's nephew wanted the house, so he could sell it. He was possibly within his rights – she had left it to him in her will – but normally he would have to wait for the two of them to die. That was what had been agreed and decided with the lawyer. But now he was in a hurry. He claimed to have signed the papers for Hortense to be sectioned because of her memory problems. He had used the word Alzheimer's, to put the fear of God into them. And of course it would be just a matter of days before they came for her, so Simone was going to have to shift her arse and find somewhere to crash if she didn't want to end up on the street! That's what the little bastard had told them, in so many words.

The problem was they had believed everything the nephew had said. And it was impossible to make them change their minds.

After a long pause Ferdinand added that the sisters would rather die than be separated from each other. There was no doubt about it. And Guy agreed.

As Marceline barely knew the Lumière sisters, they explained for her benefit that they weren't really sisters at all. They only shared the same name because Hortense had married Simone's brother: she had met him at the beginning of the war, they had fallen madly in love and managed to convince the village mayor to marry them a few days later. Unfortunately, the day after the wedding, when poor Octave had returned to his regiment, he stepped on a landmine. His parents died of a broken heart and Hortense was left alone with her sister-in-law, Simone, who was then just fifteen or sixteen years old. She herself was barely twenty-three. So that was that, they had remained inseparable ever since. They opened an electrical shop, which they called Lumière Sisters' Electrical Goods. With a name like theirs, it had to be. They specialised in bedside and night-lights as well as supplying the usual standard cables, sockets, sheathing, and switches. Simone designed the products and Hortense made them. The ones Gaby liked best were the merry-go-rounds that turned in the heat from a light bulb. Very romantic, they were. She would visit their house sometimes, just to watch them going round. The sisters had closed their shop the previous year.

The two women had lived together for nearly seventy years. "Soon be their platinum anniversary," Marceline said, mightily impressed.

The rain started to fall, so they ran inside. Ferdinand put some logs in the stove, Guy washed up the cups in the sink, while Marceline left some dried beans to soak for the following day. Then they tried to think how they would manage if there were five of them. As they went round the house they told themselves there was still plenty of room. Really, there was not a problem.

They paused at the foot of the stairs. They needed to talk some more. Would the sisters be difficult to convince? They were older and less flexible than Guy or Marceline. Hortense was ninety-five and Simone eighty-eight? Old enough to be their mothers. Now that was a thought . . . They must be very attached to their own house, given how long they'd lived there. It would be difficult for them. Be that as it may, they couldn't leave them in that perilous situation, it would amount to an offence under the law. Yes, it was true. But it wasn't going to be easy.

Ferdinand sensed he would spend the night racking his brains, looking for the right words, honing his arguments. Marceline and Guy had confidence in him. But then they had seen his talents in that area for themselves.

They wished each other good night. Marceline and Ferdinand each went to their rooms while Guy put on his coat. Before going out he took some embers from the stove and put them in a bucket. Berthe followed, as she did every night. On entering the workshop they both shivered. The thermometer read just four degrees Celsius. He put the embers in the brazier and pulled it as close to the workbench as possible. Berthe curled up beside him on a pile of hessian sacks and Guy set to work. He had two bikes to fix before the end of the week. Several nights' work. Just the pressure he needed.

Ferdinand lay in bed and stared at the ceiling, with little Chamalo purring in his ear. It didn't help him to get to sleep. Right now he was thinking about tomorrow.

What could he say? What words would he use? And above all how was he going to set about it?

The poor bloke had a touch of stage fright.

37

THREE PLUS TWO

Ferdinand was surprised how quickly it all happened. After just a few sentences Simone stood up, grabbed Hortense by the sleeve and dragged her off to the bedroom. He heard them whispering there for less than a minute, then they came back, their eyes moist and shaking a little, and each gave him a hug. The nephew had come back the day before, after Ferdinand and the kids had left, and had completely terrorised them. What an awful night they'd had! First crying over the mysterious deaths of their two budgies, found at the bottom of the cage, flat on their backs and with swollen bellies. And then planning the great, final departure, with the appropriate number of sleeping pills laid out on their bedside tables. Intent on leaving the house spotless, they had planned to spend the day doing a grand clean-up. So no-one could ever accuse them of being slovenly when they were gone. Not on your life! At the end of the day they intended to write a short note for the benefit of anyone interested in knowing their reasons. And they chose the menu for dinner. Starters, main course, and dessert: pastries all round. Coffee éclairs, *polonaises* and Rum Babas. Sod cholesterol and diabetes! Today they would have anything they fancied. Only then would they go to bed – at about eight-thirty, unless there was a good film or interesting documentary on the telly. They would say bye-bye, and something like: *with a bit of luck and if there's a cock-up in the signal box, we might even meet again in Paradise, my love.* A final giggle together and an hour later, if things went to plan, it would all be over. So when Ferdinand's proposal came it was a bit like a lifebelt, or a light at the end of a tunnel. A reprieve, in any event. They said yes.

First he took them to the farm. It was pelting down when they arrived. But their perms remained intact because Marceline and Guy were waiting outside and escorted them to the house under their umbrellas. Once settled by the stove, Hortense fell asleep. She was feeling washed out by all these changes in routine, and the emotional roller coaster of the last few days. Her head drooped into her cup of coffee. Simone shrugged, telling them to take no notice: it often happened, but wouldn't last long. And indeed, a quarter of an hour later, Hortense awoke with a start. After looking around, smiling and nodding her head with approval, she leaned over to Simone and observed in a whisper, but loud enough for everyone to hear, that she had to admit these young people were ever so charming and polite. Irritated, Simone raised her eyes to heaven and told her to stop talking such nonsense. Hortense muttered that it would be really great if one day Simone could admit she was capable of being wrong, for Christ's sake! Some youngsters are O.K., you know. It's not that hard to understand.

It must have been twenty years or so since they had come to the farm to visit Ferdinand's parents, but they didn't recognise a thing.

After a tour of the house, they selected two small, adjacent rooms on the ground floor. For Hortense it was practical: she couldn't manage the stairs any longer. Her knees were so painful, some days she couldn't get out of her wheelchair. They decided to make their bedroom in one of the rooms and use the other as a little sitting room where they could withdraw, just in case. Ferdinand, Guy and Marceline thought they were right. It was more sensible.

Now they had to get on with the move.

The sisters went ahead with Ferdinand to prepare the bags and cardboard boxes. Guy attached the trailer to the tractor and Marceline sat beside him on the mudguard. She wasn't used to it. The sound of the engine, the cold feel of the metal seats, the harsh jolting and the smell of diesel soon made her feel sick. They didn't say a single word the whole trip. He was savouring those sensations that always took him back to the past; while she was concentrating on trying not to throw up.

Choosing what to take was tricky and Hortense and Simone were too excited by all the commotion. They'd never had to move before. Not in the last seventy years, at any rate. Ferdinand offered to take several loads, but that didn't calm them, quite the opposite. They went off for a huddle in a corner and when they came back they admitted they were really worried that during their absence the nephew would come back and set fire to their things. Once again Ferdinand tried to explain that no-one had the right to enter their house without their permission, that he could be restrained, but the sisters wouldn't listen. No, they were going to choose, and that was that. There were a few hours left, they were ready to take the big plunge and not take anything at all. They were grown-ups now, and grown-ups can choose! They would take the absolute minimum. He would be surprised.

"Minimum" wasn't exactly the word that came to mind to describe what they finally decided to take. After so many years – and multiplied by two – there was bound to be a lot. Ferdinand, Guy and Marceline tried not to laugh. There was enough to fill four trailers, full to the brim. They gave priority to taking everything for the bedroom and sitting room, but by the time they came back for the second run the sisters had changed their minds and kept only a few odds and ends, a trunk of electrical goods and the wheelchair. Once these had all been loaded, Hortense, in raincoat and wellies, insisted they help her up on the trailer, in spite of Simone's shouts and protestations. She wanted to make the journey sitting up there, in her wheelchair; to admire the view and watch the landscape unfold, just like when she was little in her parents' cart. Simone got annoyed. But Hortense retorted that she wasn't afraid of her. She could do what she liked. End of story.

Together the three of them hoisted her up. And Simone blocked her ears muttering: "Here we go again, she's completely lost it!" as Hortense started to sing at the top of her voice:

"*Aïm singué ine ze rêne, aïm singué ine ze rêne, ouate e biou tifoul fi léne, aïm api e gaine . . .*"

This was a tribute to the film that she could never miss when it came on telly at Christmas. She had never really understood the story properly, nor what they were wittering on about in their songs, but she liked it when people started singing and dancing in the rain, and looking happy. She thought it was wonderful. You never saw that in real life. Except with kids. And even then, not when their parents were around.

Guy started up the tractor.

And Hortense shouted: "Come on, Simone. Get in! We're taking our custom elsewhere!"

For the rest of the journey they didn't say a word. Sheltering in Ferdinand's car, Simone was concentrating on trying not to cry, as she thought of everything she had left behind; while Hortense, on the trailer, beaten by the wind and rain, was relishing this little trip back to the past, ninety years earlier, as though it were only yesterday and she was just five years old.

38

DREAMING OF WATER

Ludo got up and tiptoed over to the bed where Little Lu was lying. He bent over and whispered:

"Why are you crying?"

"I want Maman."

"She's at work."

"Yeah, but I want to see her."

"Tell me why you're crying."

"I've wet the bed."

"Do you want to see her just to tell her that?"

"My pyjamas are all wet."

"There's some more in the drawer. Put these on."

"The sheets are all wet too."

"Do you still need a piss?"

"No. Is piss a swear word, Ludo?"

"Yeah."

"Ah."

Little Lu was thrilled.

"You sure you don't want to?"

"I've done it all in the bed."

"It's alright, you can come and sleep in mine."

They lay down together side by side. Little Lu was happy. In the dark he smiled at the ceiling.

"Hey, Ludo, do you know why I couldn't stop myself?"

"No."

"Because in my dream I was in the sea and the water was warm and I didn't need armbands because I could swim, with my head under water, and my eyes could see just like usual and I could swim like the big fishes and I was playing with them, they were really kind, it was like they were my best friends and then afterwards I don't know why, I think I drank too much water, and I weed in the water."

"I know. Happens to me in the swimming pool sometimes."

A pause.

"Ludo?"

"Mm?"

"You asleep?"

"Mm almost."

"You know, Auntie Gaby, she was in the dream too. She was swimming with me and we were both playing with the big fishes."

"Really?"

"Yeah."

"And did she talk to you?"

"A bit."

"What did she say?"

"I dunno."

"Try to remember."

"It was in my dream. I'm trying, but I can't remember."

Ludo turned over abruptly, buried his head under the covers, and muttered, "That's rubbish!"

His heart in a thousand pieces.

39

HORTENSE'S TIRED OLD HEART

Hortense had been bedridden since their arrival at the farm. The cold went to her chest and she had difficulty breathing. Gérard had called in the day before, and said that if there was no improvement in the next forty-eight hours she would need to be admitted to hospital. In the meantime he prescribed a course of treatment, with injections morning and evening. They would have to get the nurse to come out or manage themselves. It wasn't rocket science. Before leaving, he wanted to be clear: even if there was an improvement, they shouldn't have any illusions, it would only be temporary. Hortense's heart was old and tired.

What with nursing Hortense, the new house and all these upheavals, Simone was like a cat on a hot tin roof. That morning Guy offered to give the first injection. Simone warned him that Hortense might well send him packing. When it came to pain she was a real wimp, she couldn't stand needles. And of course things didn't go well. Hortense began by crying, then she wanted to do a deal, and very soon started to insult him. When finally he approached her with the syringe, she tried to hit him. He inserted the needle as best he could, a bit any old how.

She called for Simone to help, begged her not to leave her alone with this cowardly monster, who was trying to bump her off. A few minutes later the haematoma caused by the injection had spread to her whole leg. Simone went berserk, calling Guy a psychopath.

In a sulk, he decided to leave the others to sort out the two women and instead concentrate on working out a schedule. He carefully cross-ruled a sheet of paper, with columns for the times when Hortense had her medication and temperature taken. And he decided to call it *Organigran*, not a very pretty title but it was his little revenge and it made him chuckle. Meanwhile Ferdinand was making tea and coffee for breakfast, wondering if they had messed up when they decided to bring these two old birds here. It was a huge responsibility; he hadn't foreseen all the health problems. He was kicking himself.

The atmosphere was tense. They pondered the problem as they sipped their tea and coffee. The two cats and the dog realised that now was not the right time to beg for scraps from breakfast. They lay quietly by the stove. The two cats watched the rain falling through the windows, while Berthe yawned and flopped down on the tiled floor, before falling into a light sleep. She dreamed it was summer and she was walking outside. The weather was hot. Suddenly she saw something moving in the distance, over in the long grass, she started to run, and panting, let out a groan.

Mo-je was irritated by all this. He decided to take a turn

round the attic and on his way out jumped on the dog's back, sticking his claws into her. Chamalo followed suit.

Guy, Marceline and Ferdinand all raised their heads simultaneously. They had an idea. The same perhaps? But they each decided not to mention it to the others for the time being. Instead they preferred to set aside the day for reflection, think about things carefully, weigh up the pros and cons, and explore the arguments first. There was no rush: there had been enough disasters already.

About eleven o'clock Marceline came back from the garden, looking for the two men to explain her plan, but they were nowhere to be found. She changed the water for the beans, put them on to boil with a pinch of baking soda (to prevent wind) and went to knock on the Lumière sisters' door. Simone was delighted to see her. She whispered that Hortense had finally gone to sleep and took advantage of this visit to rush off to the loo. She liked to take her time in the smallest room, listening to the radio, and doing the crossword; it was her break for the day. After a quarter of an hour, as she had still not returned, Marceline tiptoed out of the room, leaving the door open in case Hortense awoke, and went back to the kitchen. She glanced at the *Organigran* schedule pinned to the door: Guy had put her down for the four to six shift. This didn't suit her, so she swapped with Ferdinand.

Ferdinand phoned before midday to say there was no point in waiting: he and Guy had met some mates at the café, they were going to have lunch together. That was fine. Simone was already sitting with a plate in front of her; she was ravenously hungry. Between mouthfuls she told Marceline that Hortense would like them to have coffee in her room, as she had something important to say. Marceline asked if she knew what it was about. Simone replied a bit abruptly that she would find out all in good time. She hated talking with her mouth full. It was dangerous, the food could go down the wrong way and she might choke. That would be the final straw.

Hortense paused between words to catch her breath. It was painful. To make it easier Simone finished the sentences for her, adding her own running commentary. She's trying to say that it's very kind of you to have given us both a roof here. Not everyone would have done such a thing, that's for sure. Also ... she didn't have any illusions about her health, but if things got worse she wanted to be sure they would help Simone take the decision to send ... the last words were drowned out by a terrible fit of coughing and this time Simone didn't help her to finish. In any case they had understood: she would prefer to end her days in hospital. With tears in her eyes, Simone kissed her on the forehead.

"Yes, yes, Hortense dear. We'll do as you say. But now you must rest. It's not your time yet. I'd know if it was, come on."

At two o'clock Marceline took her turn on duty.

Simone could go and have a rest. Or, if she preferred, spend some time in the loo doing the crossword.

40

MURIEL IS KNACKERED

The teacher came back in, frowning and looking suspicious. The students carried on working as if nothing had happened. Muriel pursed her lips and hunched her shoulders. It was the third time that week she'd forgotten to switch off her mobile during lessons. If the teacher found out it was her phone beeping again, she was quite capable of chucking her out. Her marks hadn't been that great either, so she'd have had it. Hopefully the idiot who sent the message wouldn't be stupid enough to text her back to check she'd got it.

She waited for the dinner break to have a look. It was a text from Mireille, her boss at the restaurant. She was offering her some work the following day, Saturday, from two until late. R.S.V.P. urgent. It was bound to be a two a.m. job like last time, Muriel told herself. Pity, she was knackered. No special reason, it was just that right now she wanted to sleep all the time. Even during lessons it was like that. So she had planned to make the most of this weekend – the last before she vacated her room – by doing nothing at all. Stay in bed, chill, listen to music, and catch up on sleep. Mess around and no way touch her college books. But she needed the cash and she had to look for a new place to live, if she wasn't going to end up on the street. Fucking hell. Just one week till the Christmas holidays. If she didn't find anything she'd be in deep shit. She texted her reply: "ok 4 2moro thnx muriel". Then she went down to the estate agents. It had just gone twelve-thirty, there was a notice on the door: "Your agent is currently out on a visit. Please return after 2 p.m." She imagined him sitting at home having lunch with his wife, watching the news on telly. The thought really pissed her off, so she went back to college. As she passed the boulangerie she slowed to savour the smell of fresh bread, but didn't stop. Not worth checking again to see if there were any coins at the bottom of her bag or inside the lining: she had looked the day before and found nothing.

When she woke a bit later she was lying on a bed in the college sickbay; with no idea how she had landed up there. And then it all came back. She saw Louise's head bending over her, asking anxiously whether she was alright. Muriel, you O.K.? Oh my God, you're really pale, you poor thing. Madame, come quickly, Muriel . . . and wham! A black hole. No sound or picture. The nurse brought her a glass of sugar water, helped her up so she could drink, it did her good. Then she took her blood pressure again – eight over five, it was slowly going up – and asked her some questions. Had she ever fainted? Never. Had she any particular worries at the moment? Nothing special. Was she pregnant? Course not! Was she eating regularly? Muriel ignored the question and tried to get up. But stars started to dance before her eyes, so immediately she lay back down. The nurse sighed. She walked round her desk, rummaged in a drawer, took out a cereal bar, that she had been keeping specially in case she felt peckish in the middle of the afternoon, and reluctantly handed it over. Muriel swallowed it almost whole and thanked her with a big smile. She felt much better and was able to race off to her class.

She didn't want to miss the practical session on injections, drips, taking blood, and administering medication. She had been waiting too long for this moment.

41

AFTER SCHOOL

At five to four the phone started to ring but Simone didn't pick up. She was watching a film on T.V., wearing her headphones. So she didn't hear a thing and Marceline had to run for it instead. It was Mireille, wanting to speak to Guy or to Ferdinand. Weren't they back yet? Too bad, she would tell Marceline then. She and Roland had been having a row. This time it was serious, much worse than all the others. So she would like it if someone could come over and pick up the two Lulus from school at four-thirty and take them to the farm for the weekend. That way they wouldn't have to see them fighting and end up traumatised. But there was another reason too. They had been asked at short notice to do a birthday dinner for about sixty people the following night. It was going to finish late and the little ones would be much better off with them. She would have to stay for work, of course, it was a bloody pain . . . Oh, sorry! Marceline reassured her. She had planned to go into town. She was going to dash and get ready and would then drop by to pick up the children.

She did her debriefing at the end of the shift. Hortense had eventually taken her medication, drunk her tisane, and done her inhalation without too many complaints. She had even allowed her legs to be massaged to prevent bedsores. Her temperature had gone down a bit, which was a good sign. Now she was asleep. Simone would be able to watch the end of the episode in peace – but no headphones, eh? Then perhaps she would have time to tackle the crossword or a Sudoku level 6, to revive her poor old brain cells after all that schmaltz. Simone chuckled, but kept her eyes glued on the screen.

She'd better get a move on. Marceline wrapped up warmly and put on her oilskin coat and boots. Cornelius was down at the bottom of the garden. When he heard her calling he galloped over, trampling his way across Ferdinand's remaining leeks. She harnessed him to the cart, muttering that she did not agree at all with this sort of behaviour. It was shameful, really, to spoil all those beautiful vegetables. He nodded, but she didn't find it funny. So he rubbed his head against her shoulder and that did produce a smile. As soon as he was ready, Berthe got up beside her and off they went, like a bat out of hell.

Mireille was waiting for her outside the school with the children. She had filled a wheeled shopping bag with clothes, toys, books and enough food to withstand a siege. Ludo and Little Lu were very excited. They gave Cornelius the apple core left over from their tea, and the donkey, without even waiting for their questions, started to nod his head in agreement. That worried Little Lu. But Ludo didn't seem to find it weird, so he swept aside his doubts.

"You look like you really love apples, eh, Cornelius? You

pleased to see us then? Do you want to take us for a ride in the cart? But see, we've got a big bag, our satchels, and there's us too. Won't it be a bit heavy for you?"

The answer came like a bombshell.

"Sugar. Ludo, see, he says we're too heavy."

"No, look. Cornelius, you're joking aren't you? See."

And Little Lu sighed with relief.

Mireille gave them a kiss and then listed her demands: they must do their homework, brush their teeth morning and night, no swearing, oh and by the way no sweets all weekend, O.K.? Ask Marceline for a music theory lesson – I'm sorry I forgot to talk to you about it, do you mind? That's so kind – Mireille rushed off, she had a load of things to organise at the restaurant. Marceline set off too. But she didn't take the road to the farm. She stopped by a large building and explained to the children that she had to speak to someone; she didn't know who exactly, but she was going to find out, they wouldn't have to wait long.

It was Little Lu who first spotted the car parked further away with Guy and Ferdinand inside. It really made them laugh to see the two men jump when they knocked on the windows and shouted: Boo! But they didn't have time to explain why they were there because very soon the doors of the nearby building opened and a horde of students emerged, shouting and running onto the road. Ludo immediately recognised Muriel and Louise, the girls who had come to work in the restaurant the day of the big dinner. They were very kind and pretty and

148

he loved their perfume, he just had to go up and say hello. Marceline and Ferdinand followed behind.

When she saw him coming Louise started to laugh.

"Look, Muriel, it's that boy. His mother's the owner of the restaurant. What are you up to then? Hanging round the college, trying to get yourself a girlfriend? Sneaky little devil!"

Ludo bowed his head and muttered: "Slag."

Muriel intervened. "Don't take any notice, the lights are on but nobody's home. It's not her fault, she's down for a brain transplant. Top of the waiting list!"

They both were in stitches. Ludo, upset, ran off to the car, leaving Marceline and Ferdinand stranded in the middle of the crowd of students. Privately each of them was thinking that maybe this hadn't been such a good idea after all. No point in talking to the others for the time being: they might have to find another way. As they went back to Guy and the children, Muriel stopped close by them to answer her mobile. And they overheard her conversation: yeah, it was really tough this year, but yeah, her work was going O.K. No, she hadn't moved yet, it was beginning to stress her out, she was afraid she wouldn't find anything, if that happened she'd have to leave, change college, drop out . . . her voice cracked. But she soon recovered. One nice thing, they'd called her about a job at a restaurant, it was just the one day like, but it was something, she could eat as much as she liked and then . . . she was going to find some solution, she just had to – right, her battery was running low, she had to go, speak some other time, big kiss, Granny, and don't worry, it'll be O.K., I promise. She hung up, sat down on the kerb, hung her head and started to cry. Berthe came up whining, buried her muzzle in her hair and neck and nibbled at her ear. Muriel glanced up, surprised to see the dog in front of her. And Ludo and Little Lu, holding out sweets and looking really sad. And behind them the three old people staring at her and smiling.

So that was how they met Muriel.

When asked if she knew how to give injections, she replied that she did, but of course neglected to say that she had never done it before. To test her out they described old Hortense, just as she was. They talked about the state of her health, the type of care required, her fear of needles, her mood swings and memory lapses. Muriel listened without flinching. They had the impression she was not frightened by any of it. That's what they were looking for: someone fearless. She'd won them over. So they explained the plan that each of them had worked out on their own, without any joint discussion: in return for one or two hours of care each day, as needed, they were offering board and lodging and laundry. Her eyes opened wide. If it had just been up to them they would have sealed the deal on the spot. But first she had to get through her interview with Hortense, which was far from a formality. Muriel agreed to give it a go, and they got her in the car.

42

THE FIRST INJECTION

After preparing the syringe, Muriel carefully washed her hands. Then she put on some gloves. Next she took a pad, soaked it in antiseptic, and cleaned the skin around the upper part of the patient's buttock with a circular motion: moving outwards from the centre, to remove the germs from the point of entry. So far, so good. In spite of her hands shaking slightly. She focused, took a deep breath and leaned over Hortense. With a mysterious air she whispered in her ear that she could feel something strange hovering in the house. It's a bit like the walls are talking softly, don't you think, Madame Lumière? Hortense stared at her and shouted that she was completely nuts; the poor girl needed treatment herself. Simone! Don't leave me alone with this raving lunatic! She thinks she's Joan of Arc, she keeps hearing voices! But Muriel kept her cool and went closer still. But listen, I promise you, it's almost like the walls are singing. And with tremulous voices:

Do you hear the singing
Sweet and charming

Boats with flowers
Where the couples dancing
Make vows of love . . .

Hortense's expression lit up. And quite spontaneously she finished off the verse:

Chinese nights
Lovers' nights
Sweet caress
Enchanted nights
Of tenderness . . .

She remembered all the words, from start to finish. While she sang Muriel took the opportunity to give her the injection. Her very first. A baptism of fire. Hortense didn't stop singing, even when the needle entered the skin. No crying or tears or bruises on her thigh, this time around. Perfect. And when it was all over Simone applauded. A real triumph.

Soon afterwards Ludo and Little Lu went with Muriel to take a look around the farm.

Without hesitation she chose a room in the other wing of the house, which had remained unoccupied since the death of Ferdinand's parents twenty years before. It was small and had seen better days, but it reminded her of her great grandparents' house, where she used to stay on holiday when she was little. It had the same atmosphere, the same smell: a mixture of damp, dust, old papers and mouse pee. The children giggled at this, but Ferdinand and Marceline found it hard to see the funny side. They knew what that meant. A little exasperated, they sniffed the air and their eyes met. Without a doubt they would have to call upon Mo-je and Chamalo's help, and then wash the floors with soft soap, followed by a rinse with white vinegar, and a touch of bicarbonate. And just hope that would do the trick . . . Muriel resumed her tour. She opened one of the dresser drawers and found: an assortment of key rings; corks, some of which were pierced with needles for eating winkles; old half-used birthday candles; and some very small, yellowing, black and white photos with serrated edges. What astonished her most were the souvenir postcards stuck on the glass panes of the dresser doors. She had a sense of déjà vu. Weren't they just like the ones at her great-grandparents' house? Photos of places where, she was quite certain, they had never set foot in their lives. And yet they would have loved to see Biarritz, with its bathing beauties posing on the Plage de la Milady; Mont Saint-Michel in the mist; the châteaux in the Loire valley; or the Promenade des Anglais in Nice, with its carnival, palm trees and the deep blue sea.

Round the kitchen table they discussed the next step.

Muriel was going to try to convince her landlord to let her move out of her room earlier than planned and pay back the final week's rent. If he agreed, she could move in as early as the following day, Saturday. If, as was more likely, he said no, well then it would be in a week's time. Either way, in the meantime she could arrange things so she came in the morning and evening to give Hortense her injections.

It was really exciting; Muriel found it hard to take in. But suddenly she panicked: there was a problem with Saturday. She had to work in the restaurant until after midnight, she wouldn't be able to make the evening injection. Guy quipped that he knew her boss well enough; he would sort things. He picked up the telephone, rang Mireille and explained the situation to her. She objected a bit; hesitated on principle. But after working out that it would only take just over half an hour there and back and knowing there was no chance of any guests arriving before eight o'clock, she finally said it would be alright this time. Muriel was relieved.

Before leaving she told them she could manage to fit all her belongings in a single suitcase, a rucksack and two cardboard boxes. It wouldn't take long. Guy was disappointed. No need for his tractor and trailer this time. He would miss the jolting on the road, the hard metal seats, and the smell of diesel . . . Shame, he would have enjoyed that.

43

NAMING OF CATS

After dinner, Guy put the children to bed. Little Lu asked him to read his favourite book, but after just a few pages he was out like a light. Ludo knew the story off by heart; he didn't want to hear it again. Anyway, he didn't need people to read him stories; he was big enough to read all by himself. He didn't need to be cuddled at bedtime. Just as Guy was about to close the door, he asked whether he could go with him to the cemetery the following morning. Guy was taken aback. Generally he went there at about seven o'clock, when it was still dark, not an ideal time to take a child. So he replied that of course he would take him, word of honour, but some other time. Ludo wouldn't take no for an answer, explaining that it was really important, he simply had to go there. It was like a promise he had to keep. A little anxiously and without really stopping to think, Guy agreed to take him on Sunday.

As it looked like it wouldn't rain that evening, Ferdinand, Marceline and Simone went outside to have their coffee and tisane on the bench. When Guy joined them they talked about the repairs needed on Muriel's future flat. They would have to replace the mattress, it was too old; put in a new gas cylinder for the cooker and boiler; repair the bedside light and change the neon light in the kitchen; seal the edges around the shower tub and the sink, and wash the curtains. That was a lot. They would need to be very organised to get it all done. Particularly if the young girl was to move in the next day, as they hoped. They all sighed at once: Simone relieved that Hortense had taken to the girl; and the others happy to have had the same idea. Perhaps it was a sign? At any rate Muriel seemed a very nice, competent young woman. They would have to see how things turned out, but there was no reason why it shouldn't work. More weary than the younger three, Simone stood up. She announced that she would oversee all the electrical work. That was her department – at least it had been for the last seventy years, and don't you forget it, kids! Mademoiselle Simone Lumière, with a name like that no-one could forget, they replied in a chorus. She was pleased by this and went off to bed with a smile on her face.

Next it was Guy's turn to get up from the bench. Not, in his case, to go to bed, but to spend part of the night in the workshop. He had another bike to fix and that evening it occurred to him that he would give it to the girl as a present. It would be convenient for her travelling back and forth to college. The other two agreed. Of course, it would be perfect if she could be independent. He went to fetch some coals from the stove for his brazier, waved to his friends on his way back and then quickly crossed the yard. Lying with her head on Marceline's knee, Berthe kept her eye on Guy and then, just as he was about to shut the barn door behind him, bounded over to join him.

Marceline and Ferdinand remained on the bench, without saying a word. Relishing the pleasure of being alone together. But it didn't last long. Suddenly they leaped to their feet, having remembered something urgent: the mice! Marceline went to look for Mo-je and Ferdinand for little Chamalo. And each holding a cat under their arms they went into the old flat. The smell of mouse pee filled their nostrils. The two cats clearly understood what was expected of them. No need to spell things out. They each jumped down and set to work straightaway.

As well as the smell, they were also struck by the cold. Twenty winters with no fire, it was hardly surprising it felt so icy in there. In spite of the late hour they decided to sweep the chimney and start up the wood-burning stove. It would take at least three days to take the chill off the walls. Might as well get going at once.

At about midnight with these small jobs completed they went back to the kitchen to wash their hands. Over the sink it took a lot of rubbing to remove all the engrained soot. To tell the truth, they were taking their time, so they could remain together, side by side. They still felt like chatting, talking about this and that – tomorrow's menu or the names of their cats.

"So, come on then, why Chamalo?"

"That wasn't me. It was the two Lulus who decided that. They thought the cat was so soft and squidgy they named it after a marshmallow!"

"That's sweet. Chamalo's a proper little tomcat – but that's what's funny."

"What's funny?"

"Sham-alo? She's more tomboy than tomcat."

"I don't get it."

"It's true, Ferdinand, I promise."

"But . . ."

His first reaction was to think she must be mistaken. Because surely he would have noticed if the kitten didn't have any . . . But now the seeds of doubt had been sown. In vain he tried to remember, but he couldn't picture the small testicles on the cat's hindquarters. Oh dear. What was he going to tell the children? He started to think hard. How was he going to justify this error of judgement? He had never had cats before, so that might explain it. Seeing his expression, Marceline started to laugh. He relaxed. She's more tomboy than tomcat. Yes, it was funny. And it was true: he wasn't very good at telling the gender of cats. Nor of dogs either, for that matter. He laughed at himself, thinking of the time he had encountered Berthe in the road, on the day of the famous gas leak, and had talked to her as though she was male. He could still remember clearly how he had shouted at her: "Where are you off to then, boy? Looking for a bit of skirt, I'll bet." It was true, there was no getting away from it, he couldn't see for looking. She couldn't help but agree with him there.

"And yours has also got an unusual name, hasn't it? Is Mo-je a Polish name?"

"Yes."

"Does it mean anything?"

"Yes."

"What?"

"*Może*. Perhaps."

"Mo-je means perhaps?"

"Yes."

"I see."

Of course the logical next step would have been to ask why "Perhaps". Then she would have to go into detail, explain everything, talk about the past, and that scared him. To pre-empt things she started to yawn, making some excuse about a sudden and overwhelming tiredness, wished him goodnight and rushed off to bed. He was left standing stupidly, all alone in the middle of the kitchen. With a tea towel in his hand and the unpleasant sensation of having been discarded like an old sock. Until he heard the sound of her steps padding softly back up the corridor. She stopped and through the gap in the door said in a low voice:

"It was Danuta who decided to call her cat that. She and Olenka. My daughters. They thought it was pretty."

It was the first time she had spoken to him of her children. Ferdinand was taken aback. He looked down and stared at the striped towel he had been using to dry his hands for the past few minutes. Yes, he muttered, it was a very pretty name.

By the time they went to bed, it was almost two in the morning. They hadn't sat up so late for ages. It did them good. They talked a lot. Ferdinand about his two sons; Marceline her twin daughters. They now knew quite a bit more about each other. She understood that he regretted not being a better father, while he knew she had lost her two daughters in an accident, nearly seven years before. It had shocked him to learn that. His heart started pounding. In the heat of the moment he almost took her by the hand. But he stopped himself just in time.

And they didn't just talk about sad things.

They also had a bit of a laugh. Particularly when Ferdinand started to think out loud about what he would tell the children the next day. About Sham-alo, the tomboy. That he hadn't been wearing his glasses that day? They knew very well he never wore them. That he'd had too much to drink? It was a feeble sort of argument, Marceline objected; he could do better. Alright, but one thing was certain, he wasn't the only one to get it wrong. He knew others who'd done the same: Raymond and Mine were past masters! And Alain and Barbara weren't much better. He reeled off some names: Youki was in reality Youka, Riton should have been Rita, and the two mollies belonging to the Sauvage family, that was a good one, it turned out one of them had balls! It was hilarious when the vet told them . . .

And so on and so forth.

They talked for a long, long time. Until two in the morning.

At the bottom of the stairs they almost gave each other a hug before going off to bed. With no ulterior motive, of course. But they lost their nerve.

Next time, *Mo-je?*

44

THE TWO BOYS IN THE KITCHEN

Ludo and Little Lu woke up on Saturday morning feeling ravenous. They went down to the kitchen, but no-one was there. No Berthe to make a fuss of them and no sign of the two cats either. They put on wellies and oilskins that were far too big for them, over their pyjamas, and went to see if the animals were outside. But the cats had disappeared, and the donkey too. It was bitterly cold, so they hurried to collect some eggs from the henhouse, a jar of honey from the old dairy and some walnuts from the cellar and raced back before they turned into blocks of ice.

Ludo fetched a large knife to cut the bread and Little Lu, kneeling on a chair, broke the eggs into a bowl. After beating them with a fork they dipped slices in the slimy mixture, pressing them down like a sponge to soak up the liquid. Then Little Lu set about the nuts with a hammer and Ludo took a large frying pan out of the cupboard. The problem would be lighting the gas. At home when they cooked, Roland and Mireille dealt with all that. But now he would have to manage all on his own. He tried the lighter a few times. When he pressed the button it made the right sort of clicking sound. With matches he would have hesitated, but now with no flame it was cool, there was no risk of getting burned. When he felt ready, he took a deep breath, very quickly turned the knob on the gas, pressed the button and whoosh! the flame lit. He breathed out again, wiping his forehead. He was a bit hot. Of course Little Lu was dead impressed by his brother's composure. He worked out in his head that there were still two years to go before he was eight and able to light the flame himself. A long time, but too bad, he was used to it. It was the same old story, you always had to wait: Birthdays, Christmas, holidays . . .

They put some honey and walnut pieces on the French toast and wished each other *Bon Appétit*. Little Lu thought it tasted nice but needed a bit more salt. Ludo agreed, so he added a pinch. They finished off their plates, then prepared two more and went to knock at the Lumière sisters' door. When Hortense saw them come in, she shouted with delight and kissed them greedily at least twenty times. There was so much saliva they had to wipe their cheeks on their sleeves. She asked for her dentures so she could try out their cooking. They were soaking in a glass of water beside her on the bedside table. In front of the two stunned children Simone retrieved them and rinsed them. She applied some pink paste and handed them to Hortense, who shoved them in and flashed a broad smile.

The two sisters ate with great gusto, going into raptures about the cooks' talent at each and every mouthful. With all that praise the Lulus were in seventh heaven.

Hortense wanted to play cards. They suggested Happy

Families, but she preferred Beggar-My-Neighbour. Before they started, Simone asked them to choose the colour of the wool for the jumpers she was going to knit them. Their Christmas presents, she added, with a wink. Little Lu was horrified at this and nudged his brother in the ribs. Presents were supposed to be a surprise; otherwise it was rubbish! Ludo, also disgusted, shrugged. He thought about it, then bent down to whisper in his ear that he reckoned old people always did that kind of stuff – they didn't know how to keep a secret. Little Lu thought it was a pity. He told himself *he* would never do anything like that when he was older.

They played Beggar-My-Neighbour. As luck would have it, in the first two games each of them won once, and this put Hortense in a very bad mood. So they pretended not to notice when she started to cheat, and after that they let her win every single round. It was much more pleasant that way. And she was smiling again.

45

THE HANDS OF TIME

Waking at dawn that same Saturday, Muriel stopped herself from going straight to knock on her landlord's door. Even though she was dying to do so. She sorted out her things while waiting for a more reasonable hour. By the time she finally went, the landlord had already gone out, so that was a let-down. She left a note for him. On her return home she had nothing to do, everything was packed in her suitcase, rucksack and two cardboard boxes. She had no desire to unpack her books and notes and do some revision, so she started to pace around like a caged animal.

As the landlord still hadn't phoned by eleven-thirty she started to feel really down, but she couldn't hang about, it was time for her appointment, so she went to the Place du Marché. Marceline had almost finished packing up. The crates of vegetables, jam and honey were already stacked in her cart and all that remained was to fold the tarpaulin. Muriel offered to help but Marceline suggested that first she should go over and introduce herself to Cornelius. He was a very special donkey, quite capable of refusing to take someone if he felt he'd been ignored. She handed her a piece of carrot, adding that it might help coax him if he was in a bad mood. Muriel stared at her. It seemed completely bonkers but she didn't dare say so, let alone refuse. Having checked no-one was looking, she went up to the animal, hesitated for a few seconds, then feeling a right prat, she said: Hello, my name's Muriel, would you take me in your cart? But she did it all the same. In a low voice, of course. Cornelius stared at her out of one eye. He sniffed the air around her and then her hand. He took the carrot she was offering and munched it, nodding his head up and down. Muriel, really impressed, couldn't stop herself from throwing her arms round his neck to thank him. No-one had ever told her that donkeys could understand words so well. She went back to announce the news and Marceline said: Phew!

Hortense was terribly disappointed to learn Muriel had to leave so soon after the injection. And she let this be known in the noisiest way possible. If she had been capable of kicking the furniture to show her frustration, that's what she would have done. She wanted Muriel to stay longer, young people were such a comfort: a breath of fresh air, strawberries and cream in winter. When she came into contact with children it perked her up – can you understand that, Simone? I'm sick to death of all these wrinklies! I don't like them, they're no fun and what's more they stink! Simone raised her eyes to the heavens, muttering: there she goes, off again. But Muriel nodded to show it didn't matter, she was used to it. There had been cases like that in her own family.

The second injection.

She was even more nervous for this than the first one. It threw her. So she focused all her attention on the preparations. She made a point of recalling, step by step and in the correct order, all those hygiene procedures, with the relevant technical terms and all the rest. But of course it was the injection itself she was nervous about. What if it went wrong this time? What if she hit a nerve or a blood vessel? That would be a catastrophe. To calm herself, and also Hortense, she started humming.

And Hortense, who knew every single song, immediately identified the tune. She started to bawl:

> *If we could stop the hands of time*
> *That mark the minutes of our lives*
> *We wouldn't feel such apprehension*
> *Before the hour of separation . . .*

Once Muriel had left, Simone sat down on the edge of the bed and they finished the verse as a duet. With damp eyes and quavering voices:

> *Having spent a life entire*
> *Always loving never hating*
> *With sad hearts we must not think*
> *Alas one day we'll have to part*
> *Let's not fret, but live in hope*
> *We cannot stop the hands of time.*

Hortense stroked Simone's hand. And then, feeling suddenly perkier, she propped herself up against the pillows, wiped her nose on her dressing-gown sleeve and asked for the large bag of wool. She found it difficult to choose what would work best for a scarf. But finally she went for the speckled one. It was modern; it would suit the young girl well, don't you think? Simone, in conciliatory mood, replied that she thought that would be very good. To make things easier, she helped her to cast on. Hortense managed to knit three rows before she nodded off, overwhelmed by so much effort and emotion.

46

OLD BONESHAKERS

The cats must have been hard at work chasing mice during the night. After lunch, when Marceline opened the door of Muriel's apartment-to-be, she found them each lying on a chair by the stove, with big round bellies. Too weary even to raise their heads and greet her. She started off by washing the bathroom floor, then the one in the kitchen. But when she got to the bedroom she noticed the old wallpaper was coming away from the wall in places. It was too depressing. She and Ferdinand agreed that they couldn't leave it in that state, so they tore it all off. Then she prepared the paint with the children. Two kilos of mashed potato, two kilos of lime, starch to fix it all, and water. As for the colour, they were thinking of green; boiling tarragon leaves worked and it smelled very nice, but it was the wrong time of year. So they went for terracotta bricks. They put some in a sack; hit them with a sledgehammer to make a powder, and then they added it to the mixture. This gave it a pink hue, which Ludo thought was perfect, especially for a girl's bedroom.

After the painting, the Lulus went off to play hide-and-seek in the barn. In a dark corner they came across two old bikes lying under the hay and covered with bird droppings. Not surprising given the string of swallows' nests just above. Standing the bikes upright they found to their surprise that they were just the right size. As Ferdinand went past he explained that the bikes had belonged to their father and Uncle Lionel when they were children. Little Lu winced. He looked at Ludo to check his reaction. He was glad to see he was equally worried. Because it was really hard to believe their father had ever been little once upon a time. And even harder to believe that he had a brother whom they had never heard of. It just wasn't possible. Faced with their incredulity, Ferdinand could think of no other solution than to show them a photo. On it were two little boys each sitting on a bicycle: one had round cheeks and smiled, while pulling a face; the other, a bit taller and less sturdy, was looking elsewhere, as though bored by having his photo taken. Ferdinand gave a running commentary: the little one with the stupid smile was their father at the age of seven, and the other one was their Uncle Lionel, aged eight. They didn't recognise their father, so they weren't convinced. But Ludo read out aloud what was written beneath: Roland and Lionel, Christmas 1974. He looked carefully at the photo. The bikes were the same colour as the ones they had found. Maybe there was something in this story after all?

When Guy saw them come into his workshop he asked jokingly what they were doing with that pair of rusty old boneshakers. Little Lu protested: they're not boneshakers! Those bikes belonged to Papa and his brother Lionel when they were little like us! Guy acknowledged his mistake and Little Lu explained solemnly that he had decided that morning to learn to ride a bike properly. Trikes were for babies. And he wanted to learn on this bike. Fine. And Ludo? He wasn't too bothered: he had a cool mountain bike. But out of solidarity he backed his brother. And besides it wasn't so bad to have a second bike here on the farm, one that he wouldn't be afraid to damage on the crappy mud tracks. So Guy examined the two old . . . things. Even a basic repair job would involve a lot of work. The frames were heavy, there were no gears, and all the parts needed replacing. But it wasn't a problem, he had finished fixing Muriel's bike the previous night, so he had some time on his hands.

First he gave the children protective masks and gloves. They thought dressing up was fun. Guy wanted them to put oil on the rusty parts to loosen them, without breathing in the fumes or getting any on themselves. Then he taught them to take off a tyre using spoon handles. When it came to finding the punctures in the inner tubes, it was so cold in the workshop they preferred to do that in the kitchen. After blowing them up they plunged them in a bowl of water and when they pressed down the bubbles rose to the surface. They found that hilarious. Little Lu drew circles in pen around the holes to mark the spots where the patches should go.

47

REMINDER LETTER

At the end of the day Ludo was worried. He wondered how he was going to check if his meeting with Guy the following morning was still on. He was only eight, but he had already suffered some big disappointments in his life. He was wary, knowing from experience that adults were capable of anything: changing their minds without warning, going back on their word without reason, ripping people off, buggering about, playing dirty tricks on kids – maybe not maliciously, but as though it was a normal thing to do. With complete impunity and no remorse. He wanted to tread carefully with the old uncle, grill him subtly, ask some discreet questions: Did they have alarm clocks on the farm when you were little, Uncle? Or did you just have cocks that went *Cock-a-doodle-doo* in the morning? But Guy whispered in his ear: Don't worry, son, I'll come and fetch you at dawn. And when I say something I do it, full stop.

At seven o'clock on Sunday morning Guy woke Ludo, as he had said he would. It was still dark. They went down-stairs without making a noise, dressed warmly and went out. Behind Guy's bike, resting on its kickstand, was the other one they'd found covered in swallow droppings in the barn, that had belonged to his father's unknown brother. Now it was all cleaned up and ready to go.

They pedalled along side by side without saying a word. At the speed they were going, the cold made their eyes water, reddened their cheeks, and chapped their lips.

When they arrived they laid their bikes in the ditch, pulled down their coats, adjusted their hats and wiped the snot from their noses. They wanted to look a bit presentable. Then Guy signalled to Ludo to follow him, without making a sound. They walked along beside the high wall, he lifted the ladder that was hidden in the grass, leaned it against the wall, and one after the other they climbed over into the cemetery.

Ludo asked Guy to wait a bit further on. He meticulously examined Gaby's gravestone with his torch but he couldn't find any crevice or little crack between the stones. Finally he slipped the piece of paper folded in eight into the ground by the rosebush at the end of the grave.

The text of the new letter to Gaby (spelling mistakes not included) went as follows:

Dear Auntie Gaby,

I'm writing to tell you that every morning I think a lot about my dreams and I know you haven't come to see me once. It makes me really sad you chose Little Lu instead of me and swam in the sea with him and the big fishes. Don't forget it was me who asked you for dreams. It wasn't Little Lu's idea. Also I wanted to do it, as

I love swimming underwater at the pool, I've got the record for that. Right now I really want to tell Little Lu he's a bit of an idiot. But if I say that he'll only cry and tell maman. He cries really easily, it gets on my nerves. I already wrote to you in my letter before, I don't mind swear words, I use them all the time. Maybe if you come to see me in my dreams I'll try not to use them. It'll be really hard. But if you want I can try.

Is it alright where you are? Here it's real brass monkeys (that means it's cold). Soon it'll be Christmas; I hope we're going to get lots of presents. Perhaps you already know everything that's happening here. If not, I can tell you. Maman and Papa are going to get divorced soon. Uncle Guy has got used to not seeing you any more, but he still doesn't sleep at night and he's always mending bikes. I think Ferdinand wants to kiss Marceline, but he can't make up his mind. Also, you're not going to be happy about this, but your lemon tree has died. Uncle Guy forgot to water it for ages.

That's all for now. I hope you'll soon come in one of my dreams.

Ludovic – Your great-nephew who still loves you.

On returning to the farm Ludo went up to wake Little Lu. They made some bread and jam and two large bowls of hot chocolate, and then went to see Hortense. They offered to play her at cards again. She chose Russian Bank. They each won two games, which really annoyed her. So after that they let her cheat. Her smile returned and Simone gave them some sweets.

Later they went out mushrooming with Ferdinand. They had to put on fluorescent jackets over their coats in case they met any people out shooting. It was compulsory, there were a lot of them about at that time of year, and it might be dangerous. They talked and sang very loudly as they walked through the woods to avoid being mistaken for pheasants or wild boar. In spite of the noise they made, they still saw a roe deer and two rabbits. But they didn't find a single mushroom. Ferdinand moaned that someone must have got there before them and found his special spot for ceps. They returned empty-handed.

That afternoon it was bucketing down, so they watched a film. Generally Ferdinand borrowed D.V.D.s from his mates or from the library, but he had bought this one and thought it was beautiful. It was called *Oceans* and of course it had whales and dolphins in it. While he was watching Little Lu suddenly remembered that last night he'd had that dream again: the one where he swam with Gaby and the big fishes. He recognised them in the film; it was definitely them. Ludo was annoyed and called him pathetic. Because really everyone knew that dolphins weren't big fish, but mammals like humans. Ferdinand stalled, he wasn't so sure . . .

After that they went to see Marceline in her room. They opened the cello case and drew the bow across the strings, but only managed to produce a scratching sound. They asked her to play and sat on her bed to listen. From the first notes they sat open-mouthed. It was sweet on the ears, it made the skin on your stomach tingle, and it tickled you down to your toes. Once the piece was finished, they begged for another. Marceline said she was tired. Her fingers were too stiff. To be able to play she would have to practise every day, it was such a long time now since she had stopped. Little Lu asked her why, but she didn't have time to reply – at that very moment Cornelius banged against the windowpane. The children rushed to let him in, and made a huge fuss of him.

He nodded his head to show he was happy.

48

THE SEPARATION

It had been a great weekend. So of course when the Lulus returned home on the Sunday evening, it was down to earth with a bump. Mireille was waiting outside on the steps; she had something important to tell them. Seeing her face they immediately understood it was all over between her and Roland: finished, end of. They had decided to separate. As a result she and the two boys were going to move. Pronto. Right now. She had already begun to pack the car; they must help her to load the rest. This news, while not completely unexpected, caught them a little off guard even so. And Guy, who had brought them back, was also taken by surprise. They stood there gawking in front of her, until Little Lu started to wail. She took him in her arms to console him and they both began crying together. Meanwhile Guy loaded the bags into the car and Ludo went off to see his father in the kitchen. He found Roland sitting on the floor in a corner. It was really upsetting to see him like that, abandoned like an old sack of potatoes. He went over, held out his hand to help him up, but given his weight he couldn't make him budge an inch and ended up falling on top of him. That made them both laugh. They stayed like that in each other's arms until they could laugh no more. And a bit longer.

Mireille had some negotiating to do.

Uncle Guy and Auntie Gaby's old house wasn't far from there, just a few streets away. They wouldn't have to change school or lose their friends; they could see their father every day if they wanted. They could even go and sleep at his house, in their own room, which would stay just the same. In short, this whole business wouldn't alter their lives much. Reassured, they went to choose some toys before getting back in the car. And standing on the steps, Roland waved them all goodbye.

49

FEELING MAUDLIN AFTER
A FEW DRINKS

Mireille and the children were now living in Guy's house and it was going well. Ludo and Little Lu had quickly found their bearings. There were even some things that were better than before, like being able to walk to school and back on their own. It was closer than the restaurant; there were only two roads to cross. Mireille gave in. She also agreed to let them go and buy bread from the boulangerie, as it gave them such pleasure. She never suspected that each time they bought loads of sweets. Otherwise, obviously, she would have said no. They paid for them with the pocket money they received from Roland. She didn't know about that either: it was a secret between them. In any case Roland and Mireille no longer talked to one other. They still worked together. They had no choice about that. She didn't know how to do anything else and he was incapable of running the restaurant on his own. But Mireille said that the arrangement wouldn't last for long, it was getting her down. She dreamed of finding something else in a completely different field. She didn't know what yet. There were very few openings in the area. So while she waited she swallowed her pride and worked in the restaurant.

On those evenings when she knew she would finish late she took the children with her and let them sleep over there. Not too often – she hated coming back and finding herself alone in that house. It depressed her. She liked a drink and that wasn't good with the antidepressants. After several glasses she often went and stood in front of the large mirror in the hall, the one where she could see herself full length. Then she would cry, telling herself she was a real failure. She was already twenty-eight, she had two children and soon she would be divorced. It was all over. She would never find anyone ever again; her love life was finished. She was too old, too stupid and worst of all her stomach was all flabby and her breasts had started to sag. It was scary. What bloke would want to go out with her now?

That was the reason she didn't like being alone at home in the evening after work. For fear of hitting the bottle and finding herself in front of that mirror. She felt maudlin after a few glasses of wine. But it was just the same with any other form of alcohol she tried. They all had exactly the same effect.

50

OLDIES UNITE!

The Lumière sisters had decided to put their house up for sale. Simone was sick and tired of having to go round there every week to check everything: see if the shutters had been forced; or if any small creatures had found their way in to make nests in the cupboard or under the sink; pick up the post; and read her nephew's threatening letters. She was a nervous wreck. Might as well get it over with once and for all. And besides they felt so at home on the farm now. It was pointless keeping the house, what with the cost of the upkeep. Simone would let the postman know that from now on everything should be delivered to the farm. Not forgetting the satirical newspaper, *Le Canard Enchaîné*, every Wednesday, they'd been getting that for God knows how long.

It was Muriel who told them about the estate agent. She made a point of saying he wasn't the sparkiest: he'd found nothing for her. But evidently he was more interested in sales than rented property. In less than three days he'd already arranged several viewings. He said that one couple seemed particularly interested, they had paid several visits. They fell in love with the old electrical shop. It was exactly the sort of place they were looking for to turn into an artist's studio. The two sisters just had to wait and see if an offer was made. They felt impatient, particularly Simone. As for Hortense, she wasn't so bothered. For her it was already ancient history.

So, this was the state of play:

Mireille and the children were living in Guy's house.

Marceline's place was a long way from being repaired.

The Lumière Sisters had put theirs up for sale.

It was time to take a proper look at things and do the farm accounts. Guy, of course, landed that job. As for the others, making schedules and drawing tables wasn't really their thing. But it was his pet hobby. He prepared a new file of receipts and expenses, which he named *Oldies Unite!* He enjoyed thinking up names. He liked the suggestion of solidarity in this one. Reminded him of Poland, Marceline's country. Nice one.

In an attempt to be as fair as possible he suggested each of them should put half their monthly pension in the kitty. According to his calculations that would be enough to cover the entire running costs of the house, and a lot less than each of them had spent while they were living on their own. They were surprised but thought it was great. For Ferdinand, Guy, Simone and Hortense, it was straightforward. But in Marceline's case he adopted a different approach, since she didn't receive a pension or any kind of benefit. It was very simple and in the end came down to the same thing, since her contribution amounted to half of what she produced in kind: fruit, vegetables, flowers, eggs, honey, jam, walnut oil . . . The other half she sold at the market.

Just accounting for the water, electricity and phone bills, together with the T.V. licence and decoder, local taxes and insurance, there was a nice little balance. Before they had each paid separately for those things, now it was just the one household. A single phone bill, T.V. licence, and home insurance policy. There were significant savings to be had. They would be able to put money aside, perhaps buy a . . . Well, it was all so recent, they hadn't had time to think what they would do with all the cash. It was exciting.

51

MURIEL'S POINT OF VIEW

Muriel was now settled in the other wing of the house. Every morning and evening she went to see Hortense, washed her, tended her and gave her the injections. When it wasn't raining she helped her into her wheelchair and took her outside for some fresh air. And when other people needed help, she was always willing. Ferdinand hurt his hand cutting some wood and she insisted on changing his dressing every day. He promised he would let her take the stitches out when the time came. She was delighted. What she really needed now was to practise taking blood. She tended to rush things and be a bit rough; she wanted to improve that. Her objective was to become super-professional, with a gentle manner. Not like those witches who came to empty her mother's abdomen. They didn't care how she suffered when they inserted a large needle to remove her ascites. And if she complained they told her she was to blame for her cirrhosis and she should have thought about it before going on the booze. Muriel wanted to be effective *and* gentle – she was sure it was possible. As for taking blood, Guy suggested practising on his veins: it wouldn't bother him, he didn't have a phobia of needles and he wasn't over-sensitive.

From a practical point of view, it was great here. The accommodation too. There was plenty of room: she didn't have to fold up the bed to get dressed in the morning; or do the dishes in the washbasin immediately after eating if she wanted to have a pee. She was very happy, and had only one regret: there was no Internet. It was a pain when she needed to do searches for her college assignments, email her girlfriends, chat online or play stupid games. She missed it. Otherwise everything was fine. The oldies were quite cool. But this living together thing wasn't straightforward, with all those different characters . . .

Take Hortense, for example. She was funny, but all the same you did get lumbered with her foul temper. Those mood swings and memory lapses, you had to take the rough with the smooth. And the old girl could be so sensitive! Nursing her was a complicated business. Unless you got her to sing. That was the weird thing, as soon as she started singing there was no more hassle, she could remember all the words and music, and she'd calm down and become charming and gentle. Impressive. If it carried on like that, Muriel would have to do a second period of training at the old people's home where her great grand-mother lived, to expand her repertoire of songs. Otherwise it was going to be hell here.

And Simone, who played the Brown Owl, simply because she was the younger one and still in great shape. She was so annoying. But, at the same time, everything she did was for Hortense. She meant well, you couldn't hold it against her. She was so afraid of losing her, the poor thing. And when that day came, no doubt about it, she would lie down and die, there and then, there would be no stopping her. It's like that when you spend so many years attached to someone. You no longer have a life of your own. Muriel found it pathetic. At any rate she didn't need to worry about that happening to her. No chance: she was ultra-independent.

And then there was Guy: so clever, the saviour of dead bicycles, dreaming up his pointless schedules. He seemed to cultivate his insomnia like a garden, with little patches of gardenias – which he insisted on calling camellias (another elderly foible that) – and flowerbeds that he sowed with gladioli-Gaby, a little dash of Mireille-la-merveille and large clumps of Lulus in an explosion of colour . . . Well, to be honest, he was a nice bloke. Irritating though, with his little crazes. But Muriel loved the bike he had given her. Such an unusual bike, you could be dead certain no-one would think of nicking it. Even if she forgot to put the lock on.

And Ferdinand, of course. The guy with the big mouth who thought he was being discreet. Quite convinced he'd managed to conceal the deep wound he felt inside. No but really, it was too funny. He acted as though he had nothing to live for – the wise old man, who'd given up everything – but shit, he was only seventy! The bloke couldn't see what was staring him in the face. Muriel thought that if he wasn't so thick he would open his eyes and see that his life wasn't over yet. He would see . . .

Marceline. The youngest of the five, the one you could talk to completely freely, who didn't need things spelling out and liked having a laugh. Except that, strangely, beneath that calm exterior she concealed something more painful than the others. She had become part of the scenery, in spite of her slight accent, her donkey cart and so on. But it didn't stop Muriel wanting to ask what had made her come here; bury herself away in the middle of nowhere? There was something that didn't quite fit. Except for the fact that she was completely bonkers, just like the rest of them. All that stuff with the donkey, asking if he was happy to lug you round, it was totally insane . . .

The Christmas holidays were coming at just the right time for Muriel. At last she could get up late, have a nap in the afternoon. She had some sleep to catch up on. The rest of the time she looked after Hortense, did her revision, and helped with the cooking. No time to get bored. Also, Mireille had offered her some work at the restaurant: three drinks and a lunch party. She had already made up her mind to treat herself to some new outfits when she got the cash. She was eating regular meals now, she had put on several kilos and none of her trousers fitted any longer.

52

SHELLING NUTS

Barely five in the evening, but already it was dark. Ludo kept step with Cornelius, one hand resting on his neck, the other on Berthe's back. He felt quite safe between the two of them. His imagination could run free. He was alone, his parents had been taken prisoner by the enemy, but he'd managed to escape with his donkey, Cornelius, and his dog, Berthe – that was why they'd been walking for hours, it was better at night because they couldn't see you, but you had to watch out and not make a noise, cough, sneeze, bark or fart, all that was difficult for a donkey, but Cornelius was no ordinary donkey, he understood everything, so he tried really hard to stop farting, because he knew it was dangerous, it might wake up the baddies, which would be terrible, they would get their guns and shoot to kill, they were so cruel . . . Now they were really tired, you could see the dog's tongue hanging down to the ground, maybe she would die of thirst if it went on like that, if they wanted to save her they had to find water, but there were no taps, because of the war, they were all cut off, it wasn't a problem, he would find a river, but first they had to rest, it was really tiring walking for hours . . . Ah, there was an empty barn, they could hide in it and sleep on the straw, but before they lay down they were going to eat, their tummies were starting to rumble they were so hungry, but it was great they had loads of stuff, three large sacks of nuts in the cart, they'd stolen them from a lady's house, she had died of cold, her roof was broken the poor thing, when they got to her house, it was too late, they hadn't been able to save her . . .

Cornelius stopped at the barn door and Marceline fetched the three large sacks of walnuts from the cart. She unharnessed the donkey and patted his neck, whispering in his ear: *Thank you for all your work. Good night, Cornelius dear.* He nodded his head and turned to Ludo, jostling him a bit as he rubbed against him. He prodded Berthe with his muzzle and then went to his stall to lie down.

Around the kitchen table Hortense and the Lulus cracked the walnuts with a hammer, while Ferdinand, Guy, Marceline and Muriel sorted them. It was very important not to leave any husks behind. When they had finished, Marceline would take all the nuts to the mill. She hoped to get about ten litres of oil. Ludo calculated that for one litre of oil they needed two kilos of shelled nuts, or about six kilos of unshelled nuts. Knowing that in one evening they could manage . . . Oh crap, at this rate they'd be doing it till Christmas!

As they cracked the shells they played the Yes or No game. The children asked the questions. Of course when it came to Hortense's turn, she always lost. They found that hilarious. But she started to get annoyed. Simone rolled her eyes, busying herself with her pile of walnuts. She really wanted them to switch games before things turned nasty.

"So, Muriel, are you happy with your new house?"

"Totally."

"Ferdinand, do you like plum wine?"

"Sure."

"Uncle Guy, do you sleep much at night?"

"Not much."

"Marceline, do you think Ferdinand is kind?"

"Very."

"Simone, are you a bit very old?"

"Er, very."

"Hortense, do you like eating what we cook?"

"Yes, of course I do."

"Yes! You said yes!" The children were in stitches, Hortense in a rage.

"It's so stupid this game. Can't you ask some more intelligent questions? You seem to enjoy making me lose. Unbelievable!"

53

THE WALKING STICK (PART TWO)

Ferdinand was planning to walk over to the restaurant to say hello to Roland. It was a while since he'd had any news. Roland wasn't answering his phone and never returned calls, even if you left messages on the machine. When he asked Mireille if he was alright, she was evasive: I think so, I don't know, give him a ring, he can tell you himself. That worried him.

He pushed open the door and the bell rang. Nothing. Not a sound from the kitchen. At the foot of the stairs leading to the flat, he called out, but there was no reply. He told himself he would go and have a drink in the café across the square and wait for his son to return. He couldn't have gone far, he wouldn't have left the door open otherwise. And indeed, there was Roland, sitting on the terrace of the other café smoking a cigarette. Ferdinand stared. The idiot had been on at him for years about smoking his pipe once a day and now here he was, fag in hand and a full ashtray on the table! A glass of white wine beside it. Plonk, no doubt: it was the only white he had, the guy from the other café. That was something else! He crossed the square to join him. Roland didn't see him coming, he was too busy eyeing up a young woman in high heels who was tottering over towards his table. As she passed, she stumbled and fell. He went to help her up but she sent him packing and stormed off swearing like a trooper. Get your hands off me, you big bastard, or I'll smash your face in!

Ferdinand sat down beside him.

"Nice stick. But you know if you carry on like that, you're going to cause an accident."

"Ha ha. But what brings you here, P'pa? I didn't see you arrive."

"I came to say hello."

"That's nice."

"You haven't answered your phone for days, I was starting to get worried."

"Nice of you to be concerned."

"It's only natural, son."

He cleared his throat.

"Everything O.K., otherwise?"

"Yes, why do you ask?"

"No reason. So, you've decided to try out the opposition?"

"That's right."

"That white's horrible, isn't it?"

"No, it's disgusting."

"Yeah, just as I thought."

Nevertheless they ordered another couple of glasses each, just to keep on good terms with the neighbours. Then after a quick "See you, Paulo," in the direction of the owner, they returned to the restaurant. And there Roland went to fetch a bottle of Chablis, invited Ferdinand to sit down at a table, and filled two glasses. They both gave a big sigh: finally, a good one, this was much more like it, for Christ's sake!

Ferdinand informed Roland that he planned to make a codicil to his will. In the event of anything happening to him he wanted Guy, Marceline, Simone and Hortense to be able to carry on living happily at the farm. In short he wanted them to have a life interest. Seems right, don't you think? Roland agreed, he thought so too. In any case he reckoned he'd already had his share of the inheritance with the restaurant when Henriette died. As for the farm, he preferred not to say so in front of his father so as not to hurt his feelings, but he didn't give a shit. On the other hand it might cause problems with Lionel? No, Ferdinand had already talked on the phone with him and the boy from down under had no objection. He had suspected as much, but Lionel had been very honest and said that he didn't give a shit about the farm. Oh right, Lionel had said that, had he? "Foc ze farm" was the expression he used. So it was perfect, all settled. Now they could talk about other things.

Not easy at first. It started with a few sighs and suppose sos. But finally it came out.

Not easy being all on your own, hey? Sure wasn't. He knew a bit about that, did Ferdinand. You wake up with nobody there. You go to bed at night and there's no-one. You ask yourself some days whether there's any point in carrying on slaving away like a fool. And yeah . . . he sighed. Silence. Another swig of wine. Another sigh. Ferdinand thought it was time to give him some advice. The usual stuff: children, work and all that. Roland counted the flies on the ceiling. As they finished the bottle Ferdinand's tone changed; he became animated, excited, and suggested winning Mireille back. But Roland sniggered bitterly and shook his head, looking totally disillusioned. So, Ferdinand went on, if it was all over this time around, too bad, he had to move on, do something. He didn't need to be on his own. He could go out in the evening, go dancing or clubbing; shit, it didn't have to all stop there. There were plenty more fish in the sea. Roland got up. Speak for yourself, P'pa, he shot back, before going down to the cellar to fetch another bottle.

"What a bloody idiot!" muttered Ferdinand, who couldn't see what his son was on about.

After the second bottle, Roland felt peckish. He asked Ferdinand to have dinner with him. The restaurant was closed that day: they were free to do as they wanted. So for a starter . . . he opened the fridge door and glanced inside. How about a cassolette of snails with nettle butter, do you fancy that? Followed by a small haunch of wild boar, marinated in champagne, roasted in the oven and served with a panful of ceps? At this Ferdinand pulled a face. "Where do you get your ceps from?" he asked suspiciously.

"From a mate," Roland replied.

"Someone from round here?"

"Yep."

"The bastard. It must be him who nicked my spot."

They had a really nice time. A bit too much to drink, of course, but lots of laughter and a few tears too – alcohol encourages excess. On reflection they realised it was the first time the two of them had spent a whole evening alone together, without anyone else around. They were taken aback. Blimey. It was cer-tainly the first one-to-one meeting between a father of seventy and his 45-year-old son. They remained silent for a while, faced with this uncomfortable picture. In an attempt to be positive Roland resorted to cliché: better late than never. Ferdinand shrugged and pulled a face. He thought it didn't matter which way you looked at it: so much time had been lost and that was sad. Only now did Ferdinand understand that his son wasn't just a little idiot; and Roland see that his father wasn't simply an old fart.

54

MARCELINE'S TALE

I was floating on air. It's always like that at the end of a recital, it's like my feet don't touch the ground. A really nice feeling and I want it to last, not to come back down to earth too quickly, especially when . . . I went back to my dressing room and sat in front of the mirror. My mobile beeped, I'd received a message during the concert. I didn't recognise the number and decided to listen later. First I had to take off my make-up and change. I think it was then that everything started to go into slow motion. Or rather no, I know that's not true, but it's the feeling that stays with me. My memory has definitely distorted everything, stretching time out. So I picked up the phone and listened to the message. The voice asked me to ring a number. Suddenly I went very cold. I was irritated. I thought someone must have left the door to the tradesmen's entrance open again. The one on the street behind the theatre. But it turned out it wasn't that. I dialled the number incorrectly a few times before I finally got through. A curt voice asked me my name, asked me to hold, then a woman's voice came on the line, much gentler and calmer: Something has happened, Madame. I didn't want to hear any more, I wanted to put a stop to all the nonsense, but I didn't hang up, I got up from my chair, the voice mentioned the names of my two daughters, my blood froze, she said they had been in an accident. I broke down, fell to my knees, the voice played for time, I groaned, I shouted, the voice resumed, a major collision, no time for them to realise what was happening. I didn't want to listen. It wasn't possible. There had to be some mistake. She said she was very sorry. Please, no, not that, please! Let me rewind, wipe it all out, not dial that number. If only I'd hung up earlier, then perhaps . . . I wanted the voice never to have existed, never said those words. I wanted her dead. I'm sorry . . . it's stupid . . . I'm still just as devastated today. Would you mind if we go for a bit of a walk?

Ferdinand took Marceline's arm. It was dark and cold. They walked for a long while without talking. And then they went home. Ferdinand put on some water to heat, made a tisane. They sat side-by-side next to the stove and immediately the cats came and curled up on their knees. Chamalo's stomach bulged a little. Ferdinand naively observed that the sweet thing must have been stuffing her face with the field mice again. At this Marceline couldn't help smiling. She wanted to say to him: really, Ferdinand, you are such a charming, funny man. She almost came out with it. But the words stayed on the tip of her tongue.

Ferdinand now knew a bit more about Marceline's two daughters.

They were beautiful, they could have moved mountains.

They wanted to do everything, and learn everything. Even to repair the rickety roof of the house they had just bought. For them, nothing was impossible. They had both just split up from their respective boyfriends – as twins they often did things at the same time – they were both going to make a fresh start, together. And then their paths crossed with a sad, young man. And without meaning to, he took them away with him. They were twenty-five and he was nineteen. Marceline imagined the telling off they must have given him over there, the poor boy. What a bloody mess! What have you gone and fucking done now? If you had to get paralytic couldn't you have stayed at home, you jerk? Your bird ditches you and you get blind drunk. She was a waste of space, that girl; she wasn't worth a thing. You could have found someone better. Someone to go round the world with – can you imagine? But now, not a hope! Nothing. Sweet F.A. And your parents, can you see what you've done to them? You know, don't you, that from now on, for the rest of their lives, they're going to think it's their fault you drank like a fish? They're going to think they didn't love you enough, that they didn't know how. It's disgusting. You know very well they did what they could. And look at our mother. She'll never get over losing us. You're so crap. Alright, alright, it's true, it's not your fault. Life's a bitch and we all die in the end, that's how it is. But we're within our rights to think that's a real pain. Come on, stop crying. Yes, it's tough and it's bound to take years but in the end the parents will manage without us, you know. Right we're off. If you're too scared on your own, you can always come with us . . .

Berthe had been the only one to emerge unscathed. The police kept her with them until Marceline arrived two days later. She stepped down from the train with just a small suitcase and her cello. It was the first time she had come there. Her daughters had planned to do the work on the house and invite her round after her tour was over, to give her a surprise. She had trouble finding it. The donkey and the cat had been alone for several days. Cornelius had managed to open the gate on his pen and was grazing on anything he could find in the vegetable garden or outside the house. But Mo-je, Danuta's cat, had always lived in a flat. He didn't know how to hunt and was in quite a bad way. So even if at that moment she just wanted to disappear, melt into the ground, dissolve into the atmosphere, there was no way she could do that. Berthe, Mo-je and Cornelius were there and needed her. They were her inheritance; she couldn't just leave them. So she stayed on. For them. And never went back to Poland. She left the past behind. Some days she would work out how many days she had left. Just to get an idea. She found out the average life span of cats and dogs. Donkeys too. And she learned that a dog could live till it was eighteen, a cat till it was twenty-five, and a donkey forty. One hell of a long time. She was also interested to know that a chicken could live for sixteen years, a goose twenty-five and a carp seventy . . .

55

END OF SCHOOL

Guy and Ferdinand were sitting on a bench not far from the college gates. From there they could see the time on the clock and easily watch the comings and goings. They were a bit nervous. At four-thirty the bell rang, the gates opened and the students came running out on to the street. They rose from the bench. A group of youngsters gathered not far away, all yelling, talking over one another, messing around and belting each other with their schoolbags. The two men went over, Ferdinand cleared his throat and apologised for disturbing them but there was something he wanted to ask. They all stopped and gave him a look. Ill at ease, Ferdinand asked if by any chance any of them might be looking for somewhere to live. The lads looked suspicious. Who were these two old geezers and what did they want? It was weird hanging round the school gates at their age; there was something fishy about them. But one of the boys recognised them, he knew they were retired farmers, he'd seen them at his uncle's café. Reassured by this they conferred with one another. That was true, Kim would soon have nowhere to live. They shouted his name and he finally shuffled over. Whassup? It was true, the people he rented his room from wanted it back and he was going to have to quit pretty soon. What was the idea then? The two gents over there might have something. Cool, how much was the rent? Ferdinand and Guy suggested he came over and sat down on the bench to discuss things quietly.

So there it was, they did have a room, but what they were looking for was someone willing to put in a few hours each week in the vegetable garden. Nice one, the young man laughed. As luck would have it, he was studying agriculture. But before they went any further, he wanted to get something straight: old-style gardening wasn't his thing, he was into organic. Otherwise, they could forget it. Ferdinand and Guy looked at each other. That was alright by them. Sure, the young man went on, but there was another problem, how much did they want for the room? Because he was on the skint side. Now it was their turn to laugh. Guy said that they were offering board, lodging and laundry in return for a few hours gardening every week. Kim's eyes opened wide.

If it had just been up to them they would have sealed the deal on the spot. But he would need to see the lady in charge first. (And the other tenant too.) It wouldn't be easy. She was a cantankerous old bag, a real stickler for principles, and narrow-minded too. The whole package. They enjoyed painting a gloomy picture for him. But the lad listened without flinching. It didn't seem to scare him off. They were looking for someone fearless. He'd won them over. They were sure it would be fine with Marceline but not so convinced about

Muriel. Kim was keen. He wanted to see the lady in charge as soon as possible. Without a second thought, they decided to take him on.

Of course they hadn't given Marceline any warning. So she took Kim for a young student interested in gardening, who was visiting the farm for research purposes. Naturally enough she gave him a tour of the estate. There wasn't much growing in the garden in winter; it was fallow time for almost everything. Even so there were some leeks and cabbages, lamb's lettuce, spinach, sorrel and black radishes. She explained how she worked. He gave the impression he knew what he was talking about: compost, crop rotation, and planting flowers between the rows to deal with pests. And she countered with nettle soup, horsetail brew, and wood cinders. Rich in potassium and very effective against slugs. Did he know that a slug can live for up to six years? Really! And an earthworm? Some of them reach ten years. Wow that's crazy!

Lost in conversation, on their way back from the garden they walked straight past the bench where Ferdinand and Guy were sitting, and into the old dairy. Marceline showed Kim her bee-keeping equipment, opened a jar of honey and made him try some. He liked it and took some more. She found him adorable, this boy who was so enthusiastic and curious about everything, he asked the right questions, it was so interesting. Cornelius, another inquisitive creature, put his head through the door to see the newcomer close up. He sniffed him, rubbed against his shoulder, and trod on his feet. He wasn't the only one to take an interest in Kim. Since his arrival Berthe had also stuck to him like a leech.

They passed the bench once more, again without stopping, and went into the kitchen. Marceline immediately came out again to tell the two accomplices she had invited the lad to stay for supper. Ferdinand and Guy congratulated one another. The plan was working.

When Muriel arrived they went to see her and explained their scheme. Of course she started to sulk. It was a cushy number being here on her own. Now she would have to share her space, change her habits, tidy up, wash the dishes piled in the sink, and avoid drying her knickers and bras in front of the stove. Their plan really pissed her off. But they reassured her that nothing had been decided yet. Marceline was still not in the picture and she might well put her foot down. Muriel sighed. She really hoped so. With a face like thunder she pushed open the kitchen door and recognised Kim, the boy who sometimes worked in the restaurant. She liked him; he was a laugh that guy. He was amazed to see her and asked what she was doing there. She invited him to see her flat.

Before sitting down to eat Guy looked at Ferdinand and rolled his eyes. He wanted him to understand that now was the moment to talk to Marceline. Ferdinand couldn't put it off any longer. He went up and asked her if she'd like to go outside with him, he had something important to tell her. Intrigued, she agreed. He started by mentioning the garden, the fact that she had to do it all on her own, the amount of extra work she would have when spring came, especially now there were six of them in the house. None of this sounded very natural, so she interrupted him and asked him to spit it out, particularly since the sweet potato gratin would burn if they didn't hurry back. He wavered a bit, then told her about Guy and his idea. She pulled a face, annoyed at not having seen it coming. But, she couldn't deny it; she had been sleeping badly for some time, worrying about everything that needed to be done. And it was true things would be a lot better if she had some support. They walked along silently side by side. Just before going in she wanted to say thank you. She turned and smiled and kissed him . . . on the cheek. In fact she wanted to kiss him on the mouth, but at the last minute changed her mind. Next time, perhaps. *Może*, she would dare. No, the next time she would definitely go for it. All this dithering was getting ridiculous; just like teenagers.

So there it was.

That was what happened the day Kim arrived at the farm.

56

KIM THE WHIRLWIND

Kim was in such a hurry to move in that he negotiated with Muriel that same evening to sleep on a camp bed in the kitchen, until the room upstairs had been cleaned and redecorated. She agreed. But at the beginning she wasn't sure it was such a good idea. Sharing her space would mean having to get dressed to go the toilet; tiptoeing to see what was left to nibble in the fridge; not switching on the light at night; and not farting when she felt like it. She had developed a taste for the solitary life and would definitely miss it. But she soon changed her mind. Because in actual fact it was nice to have someone to chat with till three in the morning; to have a good laugh, and pillow fights; or talk about personal stuff, even share some secrets. So everything that might have been difficult to negotiate, proved easy. When it came to the bathroom, she liked to have a shower in the evening, he preferred the morning. Neat. She often couldn't sleep, he was more the type to flake out, and so she became the one who kept the stove going at night. Perfect. She found it difficult to wake up, while once out of bed he was all go, preparing coffee and bread and jam and coming to tickle her on the neck. Great. The bike ride to college was really stressful because at this time of year it was still dark. Now with the two of them it was fun. Cool. He had a girlfriend; she was single and intended to remain that way, particularly since the fiasco of her last relationship. So they would be just like brother and sister. Sweet.

Kim, the whirlwind. He arrived on a Tuesday evening. On the Wednesday morning he cleaned his room-to-be from top to bottom. In the afternoon he mixed the paint (using Marceline's mashed potato recipe) and in the evening he applied the first coat. The next day, Thursday, when he got back from college he did the second one and on Friday evening he moved in.

It was all perfect. There was just one small problem. The Internet: that was a real pain. He put the case in favour. The planet, culture and the whole of humanity were within reach. Why say no to progress? It was crazy not to make the most of it. He and Muriel could teach them to surf and use a mouse, help them look for information, and find interesting sites on a host of subjects: gardening, mechanics, cycling, dolphins and whales, knitting and spinning wool. The possibilities were endless. They could visit museums without getting out of their armchair; listen to philharmonic orchestras; travel round the world; or visit the Taj Mahal! They would love it.

Guy investigated. Compared to what they were paying already it wouldn't work out that much more expensive to take out an all-in-one subscription for the phone, Internet and T.V. He also looked at the price of computers. With the savings they'd made, they would have more than enough to buy one. And the kids would be happy, he said. Everyone voted in favour, of course. And Muriel jumped for joy.

Hortense was very excited: she wanted to learn to "surfer sur le oueb" and click on the back of a mouse! Set up her profile on "Fesse Bouc". She loved her two new friends, particularly that young man. She found him funny, interesting and good-looking, *ooh la la*. He reminded her a bit of Octave, her husband for just one day, eh Simone? With his angel face he looked as if butter wouldn't melt, don't you think? When Hortense acted the bimbo like this Simone would just shrug and sigh. It was trying. She was so sure in those moments that she was just twenty, there was no point in reminding her she was seventy-five years older than that. So, the easiest thing was to say nothing and wait for it to pass.

57

JOBS, PROJECTS AND COMPUTERS

M arch.
    Marceline's work in the garden had hardly begun. Kim and she had thought hard, done some calculations and reached the conclusion to produce enough to feed a household of seven people and also have enough to sell at the market, they would have to expand. So they requisitioned Ferdinand's vegetable garden. He didn't object: gardening gave him backache. They started to prepare several plots; spread well rotted donkey manure on some, and straw on the rest. Kim chose a place to plant raspberry and redcurrant cuttings. He loved that.

Meat was not really Marceline's thing; he understood that. So one evening he asked Guy and Ferdinand what they would think about rearing some poultry. Before they had time to answer, he added that he was ready to deal with it; it wouldn't take too much time. And at least they would all be able to eat good-quality meat every now and then. No antibiotics, no hormones and no G.M. The two men were very much in favour. In fact no-one was against. Vegetables were fine, but on their own they became boring after a while. The problem was feeding the chickens. They went to look at the little field behind the farm. The one Ferdinand hadn't rented out to his neighbour, Yvon. He left it fallow and at present only Cornelius used it. Kim suggested cultivating it. That would be good practice for his course. The tractor was in good nick; he could learn to use it. Simone added that at home when she was little they used to give the hens chopped nettles mixed with grain and that worked very well. When they discussed slaughtering the birds, Kim confessed he wasn't very keen on doing that himself. But Guy didn't mind. Good, they would see how it went. In any case Kim knew a bloke who was an apprentice butcher. He could ask him, give some chickens in exchange. They clapped their hands. All that remained was to find the seed and the chicks.

When the computer arrived at the farm Kim and Muriel showed the old people how to use it. Hortense couldn't get her head round using a mouse, but found it terribly exciting nonetheless. Guy, on the other hand, turned out to be a natural. He started to spend a large part of his sleepless nights browsing, exploring, and surfing the web. One morning at breakfast he came up with the idea of creating a website. He thought it would be interesting to share their experience with others, explain how they all lived together, the pros and cons and all that. Kim warned that they shouldn't count on him and Muriel to help them, they didn't know the first thing about coding, and it was dead complicated. But that didn't put them off. They thought of possible names and

Guy suggested Oldies-unite.com.

Not very pretty or poetic, but it said what it meant, so they said O.K. And Guy set to work.

58

A SLIGHT TOUCH OF THE BLUES

One evening after dinner while they were sitting outside – the oldies on the bench, Hortense in her wheelchair and the two teenagers on stools – Kim spoke about his parents for the first time since his arrival. They lived about sixty kilometres away and he hadn't seen them for almost five months. They had cut off all support. He'd done fuck all on his course for so long, they'd had enough. He wasn't angry with them; he would have done the same in their place. He missed them. During the Christmas holidays he could have gone there, but instead he had stayed working in the restaurant to earn a bit of cash. Which he then blew, buying stupid crap. Now he was sorry. Because perhaps, not seeing eachother, they'd end up forgetting each other too.

No-one said anything but they all nodded.

His younger sister was five and was called Mai (he pronounced it My). A Vietnamese name, meaning apricot flower.

His mother was called Ai Van, meaning a woman who loves clouds.

Inevitably Hortense asked him what his own name meant. Kim had no choice but to answer. He said it meant gold.

She thought that was magnificent. And then she asked his father's name. André? Ah well, that was less poetic, but a nice name all the same.

Everyone went to bed – except Guy, who had planned to spend a few hours at the computer working on their website – and Ferdinand, who suggested to Kim that he should phone his parents and invite them over to lunch one day. They would all be glad to meet them. And that way he could show them the place where he was living. Yes, he would ask them.

59

FERDINAND'S MEMORIAL PLAQUES

"Hi P'pa."

"Hi son."

"Do you know why I'm ringing?"

"How do you expect me to know? I'm not a mind reader."

"But you know what day it is?"

"Yes, why?"

"Because . . ."

Roland's voice cracked and he sobbed quietly.

"What is it Roland? Has something happened?"

"It's the anniversary of Maman's death and you don't even remember."

"Oh, that . . ."

Ferdinand sighed. He had started to fear the worst. The children ill; Mireille in an accident; a fire at the restaurant. The boy was so melodramatic about everything. It was six years since Henriette died. He'd had time enough to get used to it by now.

But he must be understanding.

Roland wasn't in good shape at present. He couldn't get over the separation from Mireille. At the beginning he seemed to be bearing up. He played the stoical bloke. Life might not be a long, quiet river, but he would not make a big deal out of it, he would learn to paddle. And as if to prove it, he started chatting up all the woman he met, particularly when Mireille was present. Now he was surpassing himself. He even made a pass at Muriel one evening, while she was working in the restaurant; she told Ferdinand when she came home. Of course she made him regret the idea. She wasn't into old people, still less fat ones. And then things changed with Mireille.

Unexpectedly she rallied and started to get better. It didn't happen overnight, but it wasn't far off. First she came off the antidepressants and drank less, then she cut her hair, changed the way she dressed and enrolled on a course at the gym. To give herself more freedom she sometimes let the children stay the night at Roland's house. And then for several nights in a row. The big change came when she took up amateur dramatics and joined a theatre group. That was the turning point. It was also when Roland lost his bearings. Things got even worse when he realised she had met someone. Her own age. He went to pieces. From one day to the next his hair turned white. He was forty-five, but anyone would have thought he was sixty. If things carried on that way, he'd look older than his bloody father!

Anyway. It was the first time Roland had ever phoned asking him to go somewhere. Ferdinand couldn't say no. He agreed to meet him in an hour's time.

Before he left he went round his workshop. He hadn't been

in there for months. Not since Gaby. He wanted to find some-thing really nice for her, which Guy would like. He didn't want anything naff. He had time. There was no hurry. He dusted Alfred's plaque, which was lying on the workbench. It had been finished for a long time, he needed to visit his family and ask their opinion. If they agreed, they could all go together and put it on his grave. And toast his good health with all his mates, at the café on the square. Momo, Marcel, Raymond and the gang.

It was a little over a year already since he had taken his leave, the old bugger.

> *Alfred, aka Randy*
> *A fine smith*
> *And good mate*
> *Father*
> *Lousy husband*
> *Didn't die of thirst.*

Short and sweet. It was fine.

There was no risk of Jacqueline taking offence: she was the one who had asked for the divorce.

And the children could always add something if they wanted, he had left room for that.

He took out another plaque and wiped away the dust:

To Henriette, my wife
For forty years you were the thorn in my side.
Now at rest.

That one he did find amusing. But he put it away in a drawer. Now was not the time to take it out, he thought. Roland wouldn't appreciate it. The lad couldn't step back yet. Pity, but that's how things were.

60

THE CRANES

It was still very cold. In the morning the ground was covered in hoar frost. But the quality of the air and light had changed. Everything felt fresher and more alive; the days were slowly getting longer. And then the cranes returned. A good sign. Standing by the window Muriel told Hortense what she could see. They were flying low over the farm, in several large V formations, all calling at the same time. Some were circling above the house. They seemed to be lost – oh no, it was alright, one of them had taken the lead, and the others were following behind. Hortense wanted to see them. But Muriel couldn't lift her out of bed all by herself. She knew that very well. Hortense whispered: please, Muriel! Muriel hesitated, such a hassle, it wasn't a good idea. She would have to unplug everything: the drip and the oxygen too. Hortense begged her. Muriel made up her mind, sod it, she opened the window and called Kim. The two of them managed to put her in the wheelchair, wrapped her up in her quilt and stuck a woolly hat over her head. Quick, otherwise we'll miss them! Kim said: Hold on to your hat, Hortense. Get set, go . . . He ran, pushing the chair down the corridor, skirted the kitchen table on two wheels, squeezed through the door and out into the yard. Ah, they were still there! In their hundreds. She'd never seen so many. Hortense spoke to them. Where have you been all this time? I was waiting for you, you know. They flew over her head. Krrrou . . . krrrou . . . Water ran down Hortense's cheeks. It was cold, of course. And the sky so white. It burned the eyes a little, forcing you to squint. Time to go back in. Oh no, not yet. She would love to stay till the last ones had gone over. The stragglers, they still needed some encouragement. In a frail voice she sang softly to the sky: Don't worry, my pretty ones. Fly, fly away. The others aren't far off, you'll soon catch them up . . .

61

IN WHICH SIMONE BRINGS BACK THE MONEY

Guy took Simone in the car. She had a meeting in town with her bank manager. Two weeks before, she had signed the papers for the sale of her house at the *notaire*. She didn't have any strong feelings about it: she was neither happy, nor sad. On the other hand she did have a big problem on her hands: what were she and Hortense going to do with all the money? The bank manager, of course, had plenty of ideas on the subject. But she needed time to think, to make up her mind. More haste, less speed. So the best thing was to get hold of the cash and take it home. He stared at her in disbelief. It would be better in small denominations. Thrown off guard he could only manage . . . It wasn't easy, he'd need to look into it, it would take time. She asked how long. Two weeks, he replied. She said that wasn't a problem. So a fortnight had passed and now here she was at the meeting, with Guy. The bank manager was very attentive, offering her a seat and enquiring after their health. Simone was suspicious. He tried to butter her up, would she like a coffee? Just to annoy him she said yes. With three sugars, please. Once he was out of the room, she said in a low voice that he'd never carried on like that when they only had their pensions to put in their accounts. No red carpet, no la di da. The one time they had been overdrawn, she'd remember it till the end of her days, he didn't behave like that at all. No way. That overdraft, it wasn't such a big deal. Well, yes it was. He'd even threatened them with the bailiffs! Registered letter and all that. They'd been terrified! They could see themselves thrown into gaol, with shaven heads, striped pyjamas and leg irons. Guy frowned; she'd been watching too much American T.V. Oh yes, you can raise your eyebrows, son, but you don't know what we had to go through. We didn't get a wink of sleep for days and nights, with Hortense. And now look, it's all smiles, bowing and scraping. They've got no pride, these people. I'm telling you, Guy, bank managers, they're all thieves, just like those insurance people. On that point Guy had to agree. All the same you couldn't really do without them, and he would rather try and convince her not to take all the money with her in her bag – presumably to hide it under the mattress. It was too risky. But she was stubborn, Simone. Once she'd decided on something . . . She wanted to have a think! And speak with Hortense, if, poor thing, she had any brains left in that head of hers. That was all.

She closed her bag and rose to leave. O.K., let's be getting back then. The bank manager remained seated, frozen and staring into the blue.

When they arrived back at the farm Hortense was sitting in her wheelchair in the middle of the yard. Muriel and Kim, on either side of her, looked a little embarrassed.

"You're crazy to leave her out in this cold weather!"

"She wanted to see the cranes."

"But you know very well, what she wants isn't always good for her."

Hortense signalled to Simone to come closer. Her voice was frail and she could only manage a whisper.

"I saw them."

"Yes, but . . ."

"It was beautiful."

Simone sighed, kissed her on the forehead then pushed the chair towards the house. Kim and Muriel helped her to wheel it inside.

That same evening after dinner, when everyone was sitting outside on the bench and chairs having their coffee, Simone came and told them quietly that Hortense would soon be leaving them. It was only a matter of days now. Hortense herself had told her this. The cranes were the sign she had been waiting for. She wanted to go with them, accompany them on their journey.

62

NOT ENOUGH SALT –
PULL THE OTHER ONE!

Ludo sat on the edge of the bed and poked the blanket.
"You asleep, Papa?"

"Mm."

"Do you want some aspirin?"

"Mm no."

"You got a headache today?"

"Mm, don't think so."

"That's good."

"Where's your brother?"

"Don't you remember? He wanted to go to Maman's last night."

"Oh yeah, that's right. What time is it?"

"Nine-thirty."

"Oh Christ! Why didn't you wake me?"

"I was busy."

"Doing what?"

"Just doing stuff."

"What stuff?"

"In the kitchen."

"Uh-oh, I hope you didn't fuck everything up!"

"I tidied it all up."

"Tidied what up?"

"All my work."

"What are you talking about, Ludo?"

"You'll just have to come and see."

"O.K. I hope you haven't done anything bloody stupid."

Roland put on his dressing gown and slippers and trudged down the stairs. Half way down, he sniffed the air and turned to Ludo.

"It smells good, whatever it is."

Ludo gave a faint smile, he was a little nervous.

In the kitchen Roland lifted the tea towel to reveal a large, round loaf of bread; golden and crusty.

"Did you make that?"

"Yes."

"All by yourself?"

"Yep."

"I can't believe it!"

"Do you want to try some?"

"Sure do."

He cut two slices. They both took a bite at the same time.

"Just look at that, it's soft and it's got a good crust. The texture is light and elastic. Smells nice too. Where did you learn to do that?"

"Maman's boyfriend, he's a baker."

"Is that right?"

Roland took it on the chin, pretending to pick up some crumbs that had fallen on the floor. And then he stood up again, his face bright red, grimacing and clutching the left side of his chest. He cleared his throat.

"Well, I have got one small complaint to make. To be honest, it needs a bit of salt. And you know it's a pity, Ludo, because with bread that kind of mistake can be fatal."

Ludo ran up to his room, hurled himself on the bed, and buried his head under the pillow to stifle his crying. Bloody pillock! Once he'd calmed down, he felt someone behind him. He came out from under the pillow and turned swiftly to face him. Roland was leaning over him, looking distraught, his hair a mess and his eyes all swollen. He wore a faint, rather sheepish smile. He whispered: "I'm sorry, Ludo, your bread's perfect. I'm a bloody pillock and I'm jealous. Forgive me."

As Ludo helped his father to prepare the lunchtime dishes, he explained how he had made the bread. First, the yeast. Easy peasy. You just needed water and flour, you left it by the stove and when bubbles came you added a bit more flour and water each day to make it swell. He had started his own dough two weeks ago. He'd brought some from home to make this bread. And while Roland was doing the accounts with Mireille the day before, he had gone into the kitchen and mixed together 80 grammes of yeast with 400 grammes of flour, 350 millilitres of warm water and a teaspoon and a half of salt. He'd stirred it all in and then he'd taken the bowl with the mixture quietly up to his room and left it to rise all night by the radiator. At seven o'clock he'd gone downstairs without making any noise, folded the dough and let it rise for a second time while he did his homework. And then at nine o'clock he'd put it in the oven. That's what I did, Papa. To give you a surprise.

Roland was moved. And to show his admiration he ate half the loaf with some cheese and some wine. He thought his son was marvellous.

63

A LONG NIGHT (PART ONE)

Chamalo was walking aimlessly round the kitchen. Normally her favourite room, it was warm and where she slept; people stroked her and fed her there in the morning. But food was not her main concern right now. She was not at all hungry, and didn't give a toss about being stroked. She was just looking for a quiet place to lie down, that was all. There were too many people. They never stopped moving around, going here, there and everywhere. Only at night did things calm down. And even then you couldn't be sure. Because of Berthe and her dreams of mad races after strange animals. She whined with terror or yapped with excitement, depending on what she came across. It was irritating. It annoyed Mo-je in particular. But he was a special case, that one. Not long ago he had almost put her eyes out, jumping on her head and digging in his claws, he was so exasperated. His nerves were on edge and his reactions over the top. He was also dead jealous, that tomcat. So, not the kitchen. She went to look elsewhere. Down the corridor and turn right. The door was ajar, so she went into the two little old ladies' room. It was peaceful and warm in there. She fell on the large bag with all the balls of different coloured wool, and thought for a second it was just the job. But then she changed her mind as she sensed something. That was it. A shadow had just passed over the left-hand bed, accompanied by a very light breath of air. It felt cold. Hortense's soul taking flight, perhaps? Chamalo turned and trotted out of the room.

Finally she decided to settle behind the wood-burning stove in Kim and Muriel's flat. Their kitchen was much more peaceful. Mo-je would never think of looking there and there was no risk of Berthe bothering her with her pathetic dreams. She stretched out on her side, her heart racing, she got up again, turned, couldn't find a comfortable position, her stomach hardened like a stone, and her pupils dilated. It was the first time she'd felt that kind of pain. She was worried. The little creatures that up to that point had been stirring inside her, now hardly moved, as though caught in a vice, pressing against her sides. The pain stopped her from breathing. She started to purr in an attempt to dull her fear.

At three o'clock Muriel got up to go for a wee. She didn't pull the flush as it was night-time. You wouldn't hear anything from up there, of course, but she preferred not to, you never knew. And she thought of the need to save water. No sense in wasting it. Letting it run for no reason, while you brushed your teeth, washed your hands or did the washing up. It was really terrible. Shit, the amount people wasted, it was crazy! Muriel's concern for the environment was new. She agreed with Kim, they had to stop being idiots, stop letting themselves be manipulated like sheep. Question everything. Take control of our lives. Take responsibility for our waste for Christ's sake! O.K. But she hadn't yet got to the point where she would use dry toilets. The thought of having to shit and piss in a bucket of litter, like the cats in the flat, did her head in. But Kim put a lot of effort into trying to convince her, as well as the other inhabitants of the farm. For the time being no-one apart from Marceline was very keen, but in her case the idea was not a new one. He wanted them to meet other people who had already adopted the system so they could ask them questions directly, it would be a sort of forum. What concerned them most was the smell. And having to handle the buckets, wasn't it really awkward, disgusting, and archaic? And to be honest was compost made from human waste really any good as a fertiliser? What about all the germs? Were they destroyed during the composting? He would help them join a forum, so they could discuss things with experts. It would be fun to see the wrinklies chatting on the net.

Coming out of the bathroom Muriel hesitated. She wasn't very keen to go back to bed straightaway. She would go and see if there was anything interesting in the fridge. It was empty. But something on the table caught her attention. That was weird – a magazine and a bar of chocolate! Where did they come from? She didn't stop to wonder for long. She sat down on the bench, broke off a small piece, and ate it as she flicked through the magazine. She heard a noise. Someone was walking around upstairs. Then down the stairs. Muriel looked up and saw some bare feet, a pair of legs, then a long white T-shirt and a girl's head. Never seen her before – some new girl?

"Hiya."

"Hiya."

She stuck her nose back in the magazine once more.

"The loo's that door down there."

"Thanks."

"I don't flush it at night, so if you could . . ."

"You don't have dry toilets here?"

"We haven't got that far yet."

The girl pulled a face. When she came back she sat as close as possible to the stove to warm her feet.

"I'm Suzanne. And you?"

"Muriel."

And just then, in the silence, a harsh meowing. A gut-wrenching sound. They looked at one another, then bent down to look behind the stove.

"What are you doing down there, little Chamalo?"

64

A LONG NIGHT (PART TWO)

Muriel and Suzanne were both sitting on the floor beside Chamalo.

They had spent the rest of the night stroking her, holding her paw, talking softly in her ear: don't worry, my pet, my lovely . . . it'll be alright . . . it's tough but you'll get there, go on you have to push, now . . . yes, that's it, again . . . that's good you're almost there . . . it's so beautiful, your baby, well done, puss . . . And another!

At dawn the last one was born.

There was only an hour till she had to get up and go off to her classes, it wasn't worth going back to bed. So Muriel and Suzanne made some coffee and toast and started to chat. First about their studies: graphic design for Suzanne, nurse training for Muriel. Hey that's weird, my aunt is a midwife. You're kidding? The last placement I did was in the maternity ward. Well, in that case you'd have met her. She's dark, a bit tubby – well like you, yeah – she wears glasses and she's totally dyslexic. No, doesn't mean anything to me. I'll introduce you. She's cool, you'll see. That's good; I've got loads of questions I can ask her about my work placement report.

And then they talked of other things. Boys – that was soon dealt with. Suzanne pouted and raised her eyes to the ceiling, while Muriel pouted and looked down at the floor. It was obvious, there was no point in going on about it, they moved on to other subjects. Music, the cinema, the travelling they would do one day. Their dreams. It was just like being friends, they could talk about anything, no need for kid gloves. Suzanne talked about weight problems and Muriel didn't mind. On the contrary she needed to talk about it. She admitted that for a few months now – and, as luck would have it, it happened in winter, layers of fat against the cold – she had been constantly hungry. But that was it, she had decided to go on a diet and work on her abs. Otherwise she could kiss goodbye to her swimming costume next summer! At the same time she might say that, but deep down she didn't really care that much. Firstly, she was skint, there was no chance she would be going on a beach holiday. Secondly, swimming pools weren't her thing. She was a Taurus and everyone knew Tauruses hated water. But Suzanne didn't agree with that. Because, she had just read somewhere recently that although you might think that, in fact Tauruses . . .

When the alarm clock went off, Kim was taken by surprise. First to find himself alone in bed; then to find the two girls down below chatting like old friends; and finally to discover Chamalo had given birth to four little ones.

It was only when they got back from college that day that he and Muriel found out about Hortense.

They were shaken by the news. Particularly Muriel. She talked herself into going into the bedroom to see Hortense's body one last time. She felt that was important to Simone. If it had been just up to her, she wouldn't have done it: corpses freaked her out. But she didn't stay for long, her head started to spin and she nearly fainted. Guy and Ferdinand helped her on to the sofa so she could lie down for a minute. When she got up again she felt better but preferred to go straight to bed without anything to eat. It had turned her stomach a bit.

65

AS YOU MIGHT HAVE EXPECTED . . .

. . . Shortly after Hortense's death, Simone started to lose interest in her surroundings. But Guy was keeping a close eye on her. He immediately spotted those unmistakeable little details. Each day she went to bed a little earlier, slept later, and neglected her hair. In the evening she rarely sat down on the bench with the others after supper. On the other hand she was capable of sitting on her own for hours during the day, without moving or doing anything, watching the sky and the clouds go by. And as soon as anyone came up to her she would get up and rush off, saying she had something urgent to do. More seriously, she no longer had any appetite. And that wasn't at all like her, since normally she loved her food. Except that for her, of course, nothing was normal now. The light had gone out: her better half, her sister-in-law Lumière, had passed away. She no longer knew what to do, what to cling on to, or quite simply whether she still had the desire to carry on. When someone asked her a question, she would stop mid-sentence, shrug and mutter what did it matter anyway. Guy had been through all this himself, not so long ago; he knew it only too well. So he started to look for ways to prevent her sinking into despair. Not easy, Simone was even more obstinate than he was. And much older too. It was going to be tricky.

66

YVON'S FARM

Ferdinand knocked at Mireille's front door. He was returning the Lulus from the weekend. But she did not appear; instead it was Yvon's son, Alain. The children leaped into his arms. Ferdinand was surprised to see him there. He pinched him on the cheek and thumped him on the back, commenting how much he had grown since the last time. The young man was embarrassed, but invited him in. They were having a drink before supper with his father, he should come and join them. That was lucky; Ferdinand had been planning to go and ask him something. They would be able to talk about it. But before he had even got started, Yvon took the initiative. He had his own plan. Ferdinand would be his witness while he talked about his son. The lad had decided to take a different path. That's how it was – c'est la vie. He'd gone into the bakery business. It was logical: father producing the grain, and son making the bread. Except that Yvon was struggling with the farm on his own. His hips were really dodgy, no two ways about it; an op was on the cards. Ferdinand, suddenly the expert, assured him the operation was nothing. He'd had it done and in just a few weeks was fit as a fiddle. Good as new, mate. Well, said Yvon, as long as he could still climb up on his tractor, he would rather put it off. In any case it was fine, he had decided to retire. Not right now, not straightaway, mind, but in a year or two's time. In the meantime he wanted to take on an apprentice. If it helped some lad get a foot in the door that would be great. And if it worked out, he planned to let him farm the land when he went; it would be good from everyone's point of view. Ferdinand was dumbfounded. He told him about Kim, a great lad, very hard-working. Yvon interrupted him. He'd already met him – it was him he had in mind. But he's interested in organic! Yes, and he's right about that, it's the future. Ferdinand grew increasingly astonished. Yvon confessed he no longer had the energy for new stuff, but that was no reason to put a spoke in the youngsters' wheels. Ferdinand wondered if old Yvon wasn't joking. But he hadn't drunk more than usual and he seemed serious. His son nodded to confirm this, as did Mireille, sitting beside him. He had planned to go and see Yvon to ask him – a bit of a favour, but all the same – if they could take back one of the let fields so Kim could cultivate it. So he was flabbergasted to find Old Yvon had a real deal to put to the young lad. Well, well!

67

SATURDAY NIGHT, FULL MOON

Seated side by side on the bench, Ferdinand and Marceline were counting the stars. Or trying to. But of course there were too many, it was impossible. It was a bit nippy, Marceline drew closer. He shut his eyes, delighted and at the same time intimidated. A quarter of an hour later she lowered her head on to his shoulder and gently rested it there. For the first time. He shivered. She did too. They no longer moved, could hardly breathe. But that was as far as it went. They both jumped because Kim, in boxer shorts, threw open the door of his flat and ran out towards them in a panic.

"Muriel's shut herself in the bathroom, I think she's ill, she's been crying for over an hour!"

They charged inside.

Marceline spoke through the door.

"What's going on, Muriel? Are you unwell?"

"It hurts."

"Open the door."

"I can't."

"Please try."

"I can't move. My back hurts too much."

Slipping the blade of a knife along the frame, Kim managed to lift the latch and open the door. Muriel was lying slumped in the shower. Marceline bent down and took her in her arms, rocking her and asking where it hurt. Feverish, Muriel clutched her hand, and placed it on her stomach. It was hard as stone. Marceline recoiled. Muriel went into a panic.

"Am I going to die?"

"No, you're not, of course you're not. But I don't understand . . . Why didn't you tell us before?"

"Tell you what, Marceline?"

A fresh contraction tore a long groan from her, rising in a crescendo and ending in a scream. Marceline hugged her. Don't worry, sweetheart, don't worry my love . . . it'll be alright, we'll get the midwife or doctor to come, they'll sort you out. Muriel turned towards her, looking stunned. Her expression one of total incredulity. It was then that Marceline understood. The girl had only just that second realised what was happening to her. She stroked her face. You poor little pet . . . She called for Kim and Ferdinand and they helped carry Muriel to her room. Marceline settled her on the bed, propped up her back with some pillows, went out again, asked the two men to find someone quick, fetch a doctor or midwife. They didn't seem to understand. Marceline begged them to hurry: it was urgent. Worried, Kim and Ferdinand went back to the other wing of the house to telephone. Halfway there, Kim remembered that Suzanne's aunt was a midwife. He ran to fetch his mobile from his room. It was one o'clock in the morning.

Marceline stroked Muriel's head and spoke softly into her ear. It's alright, little one, don't you worry, Kim's phoned the midwife, she's on her way. But by this point Muriel had been suffering for hours, it had gone on too long, she wanted it to stop immediately, right there and then. She had shouted so much she no longer had the strength to say anything. She could move her head from right to left, but that was the only form of expression she could still manage. No, no, no.

Time passed. The contractions came one after the other, racking her unremittingly. Then one that was even more painful than the others, it seemed to rip her insides. The crown of the baby's head appeared. Marceline knew they couldn't wait any longer. Muriel, my love, we're going to help it come out, now listen to me, I'll tell you when to push, O.K.? That's good, now breathe in, go on now, push . . . yes, yes . . . that's good. One more time . . . push . . . again . . . again. . . that's it, almost there now, again, harder, there's the head, you've done the difficult bit. One last time . . . that's it, it's there, you've done it. Oh look at her, isn't she a little angel? . . . Muriel, it's a girl!

Feeling all emotional, Marceline covered the baby with a blanket so it wouldn't get cold. She bent down to put it in Muriel's arms, but Muriel turned away. She didn't want to touch it, or even look. Marceline really felt like crying, but stopped herself.

Two in the morning. Guy and Kim were posted by the side of the road just before the junction. They each held a torch in their hand. The midwife's car arrived; they waved their arms and pointed out the path to the house. In the yard Ferdinand took over, he opened the door and let her in. She was cheerful, her gestures snappy and precise. Marceline was relieved. Marie explained she had been as quick as she could but she was still in the maternity ward when she received the call. Babies often arrived on nights when there was a full moon. And at the end of the week that's just how it was! She examined the baby, cut and clamped the cord, took care of Muriel, checked the placenta was intact, asked questions about how things had gone, and congratulated everyone on their good work. But she knew there was a problem: Muriel wasn't looking at the baby, even when it started to cry. So Marceline went up and stroked Muriel's hand, bent down to her ear and asked in a whisper if she wanted to talk about what was happening or if she would rather they took care of the child at first. She did prefer that, so the two women left the room with the baby. Muriel turned her head towards the wall and quietly started to cry.

68

SUNDAY

Although she'd long been awake, as a result of all the commotion, at six o'clock Simone finally decided to go and see what was happening in the kitchen. And this is what she saw: Marceline preparing a bottle, and Guy with a baby in his arms, striding across the kitchen, trying to calm its sobbing. Her instincts took over. Frowning, she approached him with a determined expression. Do you really think that's any sort of way to handle a baby? If you shake it like that, it's not surprising the poor little thing's crying. Guy took this badly. But at the same time it dawned on him that they'd got their Simone back! Imperiously she sat down in an armchair and held out her arms. He handed over the newborn baby and, as if by magic, the crying stopped. Annoyed, he went out saying he had work he needed to get on with. Of course Simone became angry when she found out the baby was Muriel's. Because it just wasn't right not to have told her anything before! No but really, put yourself in my shoes, how does it make me look? Marceline explained. She soon saw the point. She and Hortense had once seen a film about that on the telly. It had made quite an impression on them. She remembered the expression used to describe the problem. So, she'd been in denial about her pregnancy, had she, the poor thing? Marceline nodded. So what was going to happen now? Marceline didn't know what to say. But for now the baby was hungry and she still had loads of things to do. So having wedged Simone in the armchair, she held out the bottle and let her get on with it. Simone fed the baby, holding her close to wind her, all wrapped up in a pure cotton T-shirt – Kim thought that important – and a multi-coloured scarf, one of Hortense's unfinished works of art, by way of a blanket. It was the first time in her life Simone had held such a small baby. The first time she had been able to look at one close to. And talk to it in a whisper without anyone watching. Aren't you pretty, you tiny thing, you're so beautiful, oh yes you are, you're beautiful, my pet, and look at your little hands, they're so delicate, those little hands, with those long fingers you could play the piano you could, and those little feet, but how's it possible to have such small feet, so perfect, so sweet, tell me how's it possible my little princess . . . The little princess must have weighed less than three kilos. Not much at all. And yet, after barely an hour Simone's arms were already stiff. But she said nothing and put up with it, neither moving nor calling for help. She was too afraid she might wake the little angel. Or perhaps shatter the magic . . .

Kim checked on the Internet: the duty chemist opened at eight o'clock. At quarter to eight Marceline took Ferdinand's car. Marie had left a small case of samples for them during the night, but although it had helped, it wouldn't last long. So she needed to find some infant formula milk, teats for the bottles, newborn nappies, sanitary towels, and saline solution.

In the workshop Guy went back to work: he wanted to make a cot. One that could be moved easily around the house and wouldn't topple over. Top priority. So he dismantled an old pushchair that he had found in the barn, keeping just the frame and wheels, and decided to attach to it the wicker basket from the laundry room. Ferdinand was none too happy about this. He needed that basket to carry the washing he'd just done. Yes, but the cot was a priority. Alright, alright. So Ferdinand used a crate instead, it came down to the same thing.

Ferdinand's job that morning was to find something for the baby to wear. Earlier he had gone to the attic to look for a box of Ludovic and Lucien's baby clothes. A cardboard box full of memories. For later. When they were grown up. It was Mireille who had put it all up there, when they moved out. So he'd brought it all down, put the baby clothes in the washing machine and, as soon as the wash was done, hung them up by the stove to dry: tiny pyjamas, teeny-weeny tops, doll-size socks and such a sweet little bonnet.

Soon they would be able to dress the baby and put her in a cot. If, that was, Guy found a better solution to fastening the basket to the frame. According to Ferdinand it was still too rickety, and not steady enough. He offered to give him a hand but Guy told him to get lost. Ferdinand went off grumbling that he had such a short fuse, that bloke . . . Everyone was a bit on edge. Not surprising, given the shortage of sleep. Or perhaps the full moon was getting to them.

The other wing of the house.

At about nine o'clock Kim made some breakfast for Muriel. She wasn't hungry, she wanted to get up. So he offered to help her walk to the bathroom, but she brushed him aside, preferring to hold on to the walls and hang on to the furniture rather than accept his arm. Feeling frustrated he went out for a stroll and to see if the hens were alright. He greeted Cornelius, who was just going out, and decided he would do some work in the garden. He really needed to let off steam.

On her return from the chemist Marceline dropped in to see Muriel. She was sitting near the stove with Chamalo on her knees, playing with the little kittens. Marceline found this disturbing. So she sat down beside her and they chatted about this and that. But Muriel didn't ask a single question about the baby. Marceline told herself she would have to be patient. The midwife was due back later in the day; they could talk about it then. Things would sort themselves.

At the end of the morning Guy arrived, pushing the cot-on-wheels. Kim, Simone, Ferdinand and Marceline all applauded, of course. It was a very special cot, to be sure. Easy to manoeuvre, adaptable, yet stable. Bravo! Guy was very pleased.

After much thought, they put the baby and cot in the little sitting room next to Simone's bedroom. Since Hortense's passing, she no longer went in there. And Marceline's room was just opposite. Not to mention that – and this was the icing on the cake – it was the nearest room to the other flat. They only needed to shift the cupboard in the corridor, which was blocking the door between the flats, and then Muriel could come and see her little one whenever she wanted.

They shifted the cupboard away from the door.

But Muriel didn't come.

69

NIGHT DUTY

Guy had drawn up a schedule just in case – The Organikid – and, without consulting anyone, put himself down for night duty. It made sense: he was the one who suffered from insomnia. But he was well advised to do so. Both Marceline and Simone were worn out, and he and Ferdinand had a nap during the day, so it was natural that they should be the ones to take over. The two women went to bed after dinner. The first part of the evening the two men worked in tandem. The baby woke at about nine-thirty. They raced into the room and conferred with one another over the cot. Are you going to take her? No, go on, you take her. Don't you think ... ? No, let's see. In the end it was Ferdinand who took the baby in his arms. And he walked back and forth across the kitchen until the bottle was ready. Guy followed the instructions that Marceline had left. It all went well, he didn't break or spill anything, the temperature was perfect and the baby didn't cry for long. But a few minutes later things became more complicated. After a long and painful struggle the infant's little stomach suddenly emitted a sound out of all proportion to its size, like a sink suddenly emptying. They were almost overpowered by the smell. Huge anxiety. They would have to change the nappy. Neither Guy nor Ferdinand had ever done this. Guy had never had a child, and while Ferdinand did have two sons, he had never found himself in a situation where he'd needed to; his wife always took care of everything. But now they were on their own and would just have to manage. It took them a quarter of an hour. Eventually the little one went off to sleep and they could breathe again.

Collapsed on the sitting-room sofa, they kept the telly switched off, so they would be sure to hear any noise coming from the baby's room. And as the full moon was shining brightly into the room, they also didn't switch on the light. After a long silence they started to whisper.

"Are you alright?"

"Yep, fine. And you?"

"I'm O.K."

"Mm."

"I was wondering, you don't have any regrets?"

"None at all."

"Sure?"

"Quite sure."

"Lotta people, eh?"

"Yeah."

"You'd never have guessed."

"Never."

"It's full of life."

"Sure is. Full of life – and it's great. There's new blood now."

"Pff. Stop it, you'll make me laugh."

"Sh, you'll wake the little one."

"It's alright, I'll stop."

"So, Ferdinand?"

"What?"

"Nothing."

"It's funny, really, sometimes you think you've missed out and then wham!"

"Yeah, it's crazy."

"Just think."

"Mm."

Towards midnight they sprang to their feet at the first sound of mewling. This time round they had the hang of things. They could do the bottle standing on their head, and the nappy change took ten minutes at the most. Real pros. After that Ferdinand went up to bed. Left alone to handle things, at first Guy got in a bit of a sweat. But that soon passed. He congratulated himself on having made the cot-on-wheels. He could take the baby into the kitchen, prepare the bottle with one hand and rock her with the other. And then the magic moment, where he sat in the armchair and realised that for the first time in his life he was bottle-feeding a one-day-old baby. He could watch it and whisper to it without anyone else around. Just the child and him. Good night, little lady . . . do you realise it's already your birthday, one whole day, but, you listen really well, don't you, oh yes they're new all these sounds, it's so interesting, you're really gorgeous you know, yes you are, and look at those little hands, they're so delicate those little hands, with those long fingers you could play the piano you could, and those little feet, but how can anyone have such little feet, so perfect, so sweet, tell me how is it possible, my princess . . .

70

MONDAY MORNING ETC.

Monday morning.

Still feeling a little spaced out, Kim went down to make some coffee and have a shower. But the coffee was already made and there was someone in the shower. Twenty minutes before he had to leave, it was a bit tight. To save time he went back upstairs to fetch his clothes and his college bag and then came back down again. There was no noise coming from the bathroom any more, he imagined Muriel was taking her time: drying her hair, looking at herself in the mirror and putting cream on her face. While he waited he poured himself a coffee and drank it standing by the stove. Ten minutes later Muriel emerged from her bedroom, dressed, made up, and with her hair done. Kim remained glued to the spot.

"What are you doing?"

"It's me should be asking you that. Have you seen the time? Haven't you had your shower yet?"

"I thought . . ."

"Get a move on. You'll be late."

After mounting his bicycle, Kim hesitated. There was a light on in the main kitchen. Muriel was a bit ahead of him, so he made up his mind, rested his bike against the wall, and went in to let them know they were off to college. And just to make sure they understood, he added: Muriel and me, we're off. And he slammed the door. Marceline and Simone were left speechless.

Monday afternoon.

After two hours in the garden Marceline returned. Worried about leaving Simone alone for too long in charge of the baby. But everything was going fine. Simone was very organised; you'd have thought she'd been doing it all her life. Bottles, nappies, cuddles, bathing, she managed it all perfectly. Also, during the periods when the baby was asleep, she no longer watched telly; she didn't miss it at all. She had work to do. Knitting socks, bonnets and tops, in every conceivable colour. Excellent. Reassured by all this, Marceline went back to her bedroom. To think about the situation, and worry of course. And then, just like that (because she should have done it long ago but hadn't had the time), she took her cello out of its case. To give it an airing. It certainly needed one. It also needed tuning, so she put that right. And of course that made her want to stretch her fingers. She played some notes and then, without thinking, a little piece. When she stopped, surprised and still a little moved, Simone put her head through the door. She was coming to give some news: the little one liked music! She had been crying for a while, kicking her little legs like crazy – she must have colic, the poor thing – and hey presto, at the first notes she'd stopped crying! As if by magic. You know what you have to do now, Marceline, she added jokingly.

Muriel dropped in to see them when she got back from college. She had thought a lot about it: if they wanted to keep the baby, that was alright by her. But she didn't want it herself. Full stop. Straight and to the point, but there was a slight wavering. During the day they had all discussed what to do and what tactics to adopt. The only thing they could agree on was that she needed time. It remained to be seen if she would get used to the idea, change her mind or take to the baby. So they replied that it was all agreed. But that didn't stop her needing to register the birth at the town hall. Urgently. Alright, the following morning before school they would take the baby in the car, since it had to be present too. Then they were going to have to find a name . . . She told them to pick one themselves. Fine, they would have a think and come up with some suggestions. No, she would rather they decided. They didn't want to give in – it felt important that she should be the one . . . But Simone was sick and tired having to call her the baby, the child, the little one, the little sweetie . . . so she butted in:

"How about Paulette?"

Vague expressions all round.

"Nice name, don't you think? What's the matter, don't you like it?"

Everyone took a sudden interest in the lines and curves on the tablecloth.

"How about you, Muriel, what do you think?"

Muriel shrugged and went out.

At the town hall they asked what name they should put down and Muriel replied:

Paulette. With Lucy, as her middle name.

It had been her mother's first name.

It came from the Latin and meant light, or lumière.

Thanks

Thanks to Florence Sultan for her support, patience and that so attractive, slightly husky voice.

Also, of course, to Adeline Vanot, Christelle Pestana, Patricia Roussel, Virginie Ebat and Hélène Kloeckner.

The song quoted on page 151 is "Nuits de Chine", lyrics by Ernest Dumont.

The song quoted on page 166 is "Arrêter les aiguilles", lyrics by Paul Briollet/Paul Dalbret.

The website – Oldies Unite! – mentioned towards the end of the book (as created by Guy, Ferdinand, Marceline, Simone and Hortense) does exist. The site's French name is: solidarvioc.com

Thanks to Étienne Kraeutler for acting as Webmaster and to Camille Constantine for her help with the graphic design and maintenance.

It is there to be consulted, added to, commented upon, and criticised (ouch! Do go easy, though . . .) As the name suggests, the site discusses solidarity between generations, between young and old.

BARBARA CONSTANTINE was born in Nice, France, in 1955. She is a scriptwriter and ceramicist as well as a writer of novels for adults and young adults. *And Then Came Paulette* is her fourth, and the first to be translated into English.

JUSTIN PHIPPS translates from French and Russian into English, most recently the crime novels of Xavier-Marie Bonnot.